PRAISE FOR *KATJA FROM*

"What is impressive about Logan is his di[stinctive?]
tone and atmosphere and his deftly sketch[ed?]
wants, and probably deserves, his own gen[re?]

"Though the story is compelling enough to make you want to keep reading, Logan's storytelling decisions here are what really elevates the whole experience. There are times where—despite the grit and the tawdry surroundings—Logan comes very close to creating something like art. *Katja From the Punk Band* is so good its almost scary."
—**Lincoln Cho**, *January Magazine*

"Readers who can tolerate the deliberately unpleasant action will appreciate the skill with which it's presented. . . ."
—*Publishers Weekly*

"Excellent prose and pacing make *Katja From The Punk Band* one of those books you'll endlessly recommend. . . ."
—**Luca Veste, author of** *Dead Gone*

"Annoying, annoying, annoying. Really, I'm appalled. This man stole perhaps eight hours from me and I want them back. . . ."
—**Cormac O'Siochain,** *The Crime Of It All*

PRAISE FOR SIMON LOGAN

"A visionary in the genre's midst. . . ."

—**Asimov's**

"Like a combination of David Bunch and J. G. Ballard, Logan tells tales of a wounded humanity that has lived so long with its mechanical adjuncts that 'nature' is a meaningless term. . . ."
—**Paul Di Filippo, author of** *The Steampunk Trilogy*

"Logan is a stylish transgressor for the next evolutionary moment. He reminds me of Harlan Ellison at his most daring and dangerous raw, fearless, unpredictable, disturbing, and much needed. . . ."
—**Jack O' Connell, author of** *Word Made Flesh* **and** *The Resurrectionist*

"Logan proves to be a powerful stylist with a distinct vision. . . ."
—**Jeffrey Thomas, author of** *Punktown*

"Logan wields a fuck of a lot of power with only a few words. . . ."
—**Dan Schaffer, creator of** *Dogwitch*

GET KATJA

SIMON LOGAN

ChiZine Publications

FIRST EDITION

Get Katja © 2013 by Simon Logan
Cover artwork © 2013 by Erik Mohr
Cover design © 2013 by Kerrie McCreadie
Interior design © 2013 by Kerrie McCreadie

Distributed in Canada by
HarperCollins Canada Ltd.
1995 Markham Road
Scarborough, ON M1B 5M8
Toll Free: 1-800-387-0117
e-mail: hcorder@harpercollins.com

Distributed in the U.S. by
Diamond Book Distributors
1966 Greenspring Drive
Timonium, MD 21093
Phone: 1-410-560-7100 x826
e-mail: books@diamondbookdistributors.com

Library and Archives Canada Cataloguing in Publication

Logan, Simon, 1977-, author
     Get Katja / Simon Logan.

Issued in print and electronic formats.
ISBN 978-1-77148-167-0 (pbk.).--ISBN 978-1-77148-168-7 (ebook)

     I. Title.

PR6112.O33G48 2014   823'.92   C2013-907736-7
                                               C2013-907737-5

CHIZINE PUBLICATIONS
Toronto, Canada
www.chizinepub.com
info@chizinepub.com

Edited by Sam Zucchi
Copyedited and proofread by Sèphera Girón

Canada Council   Conseil des arts
for the Arts   du Canada

We acknowledge the support of the Canada Council for the Arts which last year invested $20.1 million in writing and publishing throughout Canada.

ONTARIO ARTS COUNCIL
CONSEIL DES ARTS DE L'ONTARIO
50 YEARS OF ONTARIO GOVERNMENT SUPPORT OF THE ARTS
50 ANS DE SOUTIEN DU GOUVERNEMENT DE L'ONTARIO AUX ARTS

Published with the generous assistance of the Ontario Arts Council.

Printed in Canada

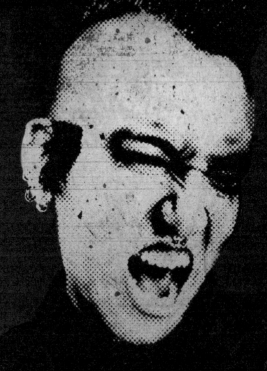

SIMON LOGAN

GET KATJA

FROM THE AUTHOR OF *KATJA FROM THE PUNK BAND*

1.

Waking up to find herself strapped to a gurney, the wall beside her stickered with x-rays and the lurid blueprints of the bizarre surgery she is about to be subjected to, Katja decides that things can't get any more fucked up. Of course, she'd had the same thought not that long ago—before the mad surgeon, the sweaty cop and the gang of hoodlum transvestites—so what did she know?

And so before the gurney, before anything else, there was the sound check. . . .

2.

With the final chord still ringing, she presses the guitar up against the amp, squeezing out every last drop of feedback as sweat slides down her face and arms. She turns back to the crowd, probably around a dozen or so people, if that, letting the sound cycle and decay, her breathing only now returning to something akin to normal.

There's a guy in a leather jacket and bright white trainers with their tongues protruding, his arm around a drug-skinny girl with more piercings than teeth; an immense biker with a walrus moustache and scabbed knuckles; a fat guy in a raincoat; a teenage runaway still nursing the same beer he'd bought when the sound checks had begun, delaying his return to the streets.

And then there's the transvestites—four in total. Their indifference to the music is as forced as their positioning amidst the meagre crowd.

Katja leans into the mike. "Yeah, fuck you too," she says, then whips the cable from her guitar and stalks off.

Her bandmates linger momentarily before following

her cue, jumping from the rear of the stage into the short corridor leading out the back of the building.

"Hey, wait up," Joey says, his drumsticks still clasped in one hand. "You want to go get a drink or something?"

"Did you see them?"

"See who?" Joey asks. Max shows up behind him, his bass guitar slung over his shoulder.

"The trannies."

"The what now?"

"Never mind," she says. She snatches her hoody from a hook and pulls it on.

"It wasn't exactly packed out there," Max says.

"What did you expect? It was just a sound check."

"But it was still on the posters. Is that the sort of crowd we're going to get tonight?"

"I've had worse," she tells them. "What were the pair of you expecting, a ten-thousand-seater arena? It is what it is. You want to play or what?"

"I'm just saying is all, " Max mumbles.

"If you're here for the groupies or the money then I suggest you figure out a plan B."

"Yeah, c'mon Max," Joey says, "it is what it is. And, hey, at least tonight we get paid, right?"

"Hopefully," Katja says, looking up the corridor to Dimebag Dexter, the bar's owner, already hustling on the next act.

"So you coming or what, Kat?"

She bristles at the contraction of her name but doesn't say anything. Shakes her head.

"Some other time," she says, turning and walking away. "See you all tonight."

She strides past a bouncer who makes a show of removing the ear plugs he has been wearing and dropping them to the ground like spent bullets. Katja pushes the rear fire door open and as it swings away from her there's the now-familiar moment of panic, of expecting someone to be waiting for her there.

But it's only the grainy darkness which fills the alley beyond, tinted red by the neon exit sign above the door. The chilly air immediately cools the sweat on her skin. She lights a cigarette and a smile blossoms on her face, sparked by the buzz of finally playing a show again— and almost immediately the creeping sensation of being watched returns to her, a constant companion ever since having escaped to the mainland.

She blows smoke into the air, runs a hand across her freshly shaven scalp, then traces a finger across her neck tattoo, the skin there still slightly flaky from the recent inking. She takes another drag on the cigarette, adjusts her grip on the guitar, then walks up the alley which leads away from the Wheatsheaf.

Stops dead when four figures appear before her then spread out to block her in. They wear figure-hugging dresses and vicious heels, bright red lipstick and glittery, gaudy jewellery.

"Finished already?" one of them says in a deep, gravelly voice. She steps forward. Her hair is piled into a dogwitch-black beehive which defies gravity. "No encore?"

Katja shrugs, subtly checking for available escape routes but not finding any. "Leave them wanting more."

"A girl after my own heart." She snatches the cigarette from Katja's lips with two manicured fingers, takes a deep enough drag to burn it down to the tip, then discards it. "I'm Lady Delicious. And I'm here to collect, honey."

"I don't have any honey."

A flicker of a smile skips between the transvestites as if it were a joint being passed around.

"Lady D has been looking for you," one of the others says. This one is shorter than Lady Delicious, stockier too, her efforts ruined by the five o'clock shadow darkening her jawline. "Lucky I spotted this."

She holds up a poster advertising the gig, torn from a wall. *The Broken* is emblazoned across the top in chunky black lettering alongside a grainy picture of Katja sporting her shaven head and neck tattoo. Beneath that, the times and location of the open sound check and the gig which would follow later that night.

"I don't know what you're talking about. You must have mistaken me for someone else."

Lady D takes the poster and holds it up to the illumination coming from a nearby street light. "I don't think so, it's here in black and white. Or are you going to pretend like you don't know anything about the money?"

"I don't know anything about the money."

"Nikolai knows about it though, doesn't he?" She looks to her Tgirls who nod in confirmation.

"Nikolai's gone," Katja tells them, stiffening at the mention of the man's name. "He was kicked out of the band and I don't know, or care, where he is."

She tries to push past them but they close in and block her route.

"Unfortunately that's inconsequential. The money was taken out in the band's name—therefore we intend to collect from the band, regardless of who is or isn't in it."

Katja bites down on her anger at Nikolai fucking her over once again.

"The Stumps are dead. I don't know what that junkie fuckwit was playing at but it's nothing to do with me."

"I don't care what you're calling yourselves, the debt is the debt."

"Yeah well you're straight outta luck, we don't have any money."

"What about your gig fee?" Lady D asks, nodding at the instrument slung across Katja's shoulder.

"There isn't one. Not yet. You think that cheap bastard in there would give us our fee in advance?"

"So you *are* getting a fee."

"Only after we've played tonight."

"You sure about that?"

"Look, I've already told you—"

"Answer the fucking question, *honey*," one of the other Tgirls interjects. This one is slender but with a pot-belly which stretches the glittery fabric of her dress to the point where it becomes slightly translucent.

"Yes," Katja says. "Tonight."

"Then we'll come back tonight to collect," Lady D replies. "In the meantime I'll take that if you don't mind."

She points to the guitar.

"But I need it for the gig."

"Don't worry, I'll give it back. It's just a little insurance on my part. Give."

She says it in the same measured, soft tone she has used all along but there is more menace in her eyes now.

Katja knows she has no choice and takes it off, hands it to the pot-bellied one.

"Now if you'll excuse us, we have other business to attend to. We'll see you later tonight," Lady D says.

An instruction, not a question.

The four disappear around the corner, and then a few moments later an engine revs and tires squeal. When Katja exits the alley there is no sign of them.

She pulls her hood up, her paranoia about coming out of hiding well-founded after all, even if not for the reasons she initially had.

With nothing else to do she walks in the direction of the squat. She takes the usual unnecessarily circuitous route there, a habit she developed after escaping from the island, weaving through the strip clubs and drug bars. She passes the tattoo parlour where she recently had her neck and chest tattoo inked—a multi-coloured cacophony of shapes which are either flames or angel wings, or perhaps both, circling around the words *When You Hit Me, Hit Me Hard* in an elaborate script. The design, in the end, hadn't been as important as whether it did a good job masking what was left of the trach tube she had cut away.

She ignores the patter of porno theatre salesmen and the muttered remarks of hookers before emerging into a quieter district of old houses, most of which have all of their windows boarded up or smashed in. The squat is the fourth one along and she slows her pace as she approaches it.

There was no point in trying to get in, of course, they'd kicked her out several weeks ago. The journey to it is merely a reflex, a memory, something she feels compelled to do before finding a doorway or abandoned garage to hole up in for the night.

Just as she turns to cross the street, tires screech and a set of headlights flash across her. She runs purely on instinct, not even bothering to see who it is or whether they are coming for her, but she only makes it as far as the unkempt lawn of the next building before being jumped upon.

She crashes to the ground and feels the weight of someone pushing down on her. Something soft is pressed to her face, a rag or cloth, and then the smell hits her. Chemical-rich and heady, her vision instantly begins to sparkle. She struggles but already her limbs are disobeying her. Everything is slowing down.

She manages to turn onto her back, her assailant a vast shadow haloed by the streetlights behind them.

His face only becomes clear when he leans in close enough for her to smell the tequila on his breath—fat, a handlebar moustache and bulging eyes.

"Stop fucking *fighting*, you little tramp," he sneers at her in an accent she can't quite place.

Darkness gathers at the edge of Katja's vision, then closes in around her. She feels herself starting to drift, focuses on the streetlight to maintain her consciousness.

"I know who you are, Katja," the man says, grinning madly. "And I think we both know there are certain people who would just love to get their hands on you."

3.

A wave of disbelief slams into DeBoer as he stares down at the cards Frank has just turned over. He had been certain he had the man beaten this time. Certain.

He looks back and forth from his cards to Frank's, aware of the others gathered around the table smiling in schadenfreude. Their expressions are reflected in the mirrors which line one entire wall of the barbershop, white flashes of teeth floating in the dim light next to the chrome of the cutting chairs.

"One more," DeBoer says, licking his lips and running a hand through his oil-slicked hair.

"No more," Frank tells him.

He doesn't even bother to drag his winnings towards him, just leaving them there in the middle of the table as if to tempt DeBoer into grabbing them back. The others get up, stuffing their own winnings into the pockets and finishing the last of their drinks and cigars.

"Just one more game."

"And what do you propose to play with?" Frank asks

him, pushing the table they had been playing at back to its usual place against the rear wall.

"I can get more money."

"You're already in the hole for twenty G."

"So what? Water over a duck's bridge. Just give me a chance to win it back, Frank."

Frank gets up and places a hand on DeBoer's shoulder, a gesture which should feel far more friendly than it actually does. It smells strongly of Barbicide and shaving foam. "Your trouble, DeBoer, is that you don't know when to stop digging."

He pats DeBoer then stacks the last of the chairs up next to the table. "Same time next week boys?"

The others murmur in agreement as they leave. The pile of cash and paper I.O.U.'s remain on the table before DeBoer. Sweat beads on his upper lip and he licks it away, unable to take his eyes from the loot.

"Can you give me a few days?" he asks.

"No," Frank tells him, now clearing up the glasses and empty liquor bottles. "Twenty-four hours, same as always."

"And if I don't?" DeBoer asks with forced bravado. "What you going to do—call the cops?"

He laughs nervously. Frank smiles and stands before DeBoer.

"No, Detective," he says. "I'll call Lady Delicious."

DeBoer laughs again, a desperate little snort. "That freak couldn't—"

Frank snatches DeBoer by his flabby throat and forces him through the door and out into the street. DeBoer stumbles and falls backwards into some bags of trash, having to fight his way out of them as they shift and squelch underhand. He picks himself up, anger swelling within him and Frank looks at him, just waiting for a response, but DeBoer keeps it in check. He brushes his coat down.

"Here," Frank says, holding out a bottle of liquor. "Think of it as a consolation prize."

DeBoer takes it, resisting the urge to smack the crooked barber across the head with it.

"Twenty-four hours, Detective," Frank says, then closes the door.

DeBoer stands there for several moments, paralysed with impotence. Then he mutters "Fuck you, Frank," and unscrews the lid of the tequila. He takes a sip and spits it back out so that it splatters against Frank's door and dribbles down in little golden rivulets.

He wipes the booze from his moustache then walks back towards his car, muttering further threats and obscenities, swigging what remains of the liquor as he goes.

"What the hell . . . ?"

He slows to a halt, looks at his car parked up on the opposite side of the road and sees a group of teenagers huddled around it.

"Hey!" he shouts, starting towards them. "Hey!"

They scatter as soon as they hear him, revealing the four slashed tires. He gives chase but they're too fast. Within moments they're gone, only the echoes of their laughter remaining, and he is doubled-up, desperately trying to recover his breath.

"Little . . . bastards. . . ." he gasps, then throws the bottle. The glass shatters somewhere in the darkness.

He staggers to his car, kicks at a deflated tire and notices the scratches in the paintwork too. He leans on the roof of the vehicle, wondering if the night can get any worse.

Then he spots the poster—and suddenly things start to look up.

#

DeBoer scratches his ass crack as he approaches the poster.

It's pasted to the wall, competing for space with a dozen or so others. Mostly monotone with flashes of red and the words *The Broken* in large, jagged writing across the top, it is the rough image of the woman at the centre which catches his attention. In mid-swing of the guitar she wears, her teeth bared in a grimace or anger, a microphone to one side. Her hair emerges in random spikes from her head and there's a strange tube emerging from her throat.

As he gets closer, DeBoer realizes that those last two details have been added to the poster in marker pen.

He squints, attempting to figure out why she is so familiar—and then the realisation hits him.

The girl from the island.

The girl who was responsible for the deaths of, among others, Wvladyslaw Szerynski, with whom DeBoer previously had a sweet smuggling deal on the go. Right up until she murdered the man in his own arcade, of course.

"Well, well, well, looks like every coat has a silver lining after all. You're the reason I had to turn to gambling in the first place, you little bitch," he says to the poster, his lip curling. He searches his memory for her name but it eludes him.

He slicks his hair back from his brow, reading the date and time of the advertised gig as well as the location, the Wheatsheaf. Hadn't that place burned to the ground a few months back? He then notices an additional banner across the lower-left hand corner, the time of an open soundcheck. He checks his watch—it's due to start in less than twenty minutes.

"Plenty who would be willing to pay up to have you in their hands from what I hear," he says to the poster, running a hand across the woman's face.

He turns and looks once more at his car tires. They are utterly deflated.

A set of headlights appear and he steps into the road, waving his arms to slow the vehicle down. It looks as if it is about to swerve to avoid him then the brakes suddenly squeal and it comes to a halt, a boxy old station wagon torn straight out of the 1980s Soviet Union. He circles around to the driver's side and knocks on the window. It cranks down and an old man peers out from within, his nose is scrunched up in an effort to keep a pair of thick-lensed glasses from falling off.

"Get out of the car," DeBoer says.

"Excuse me? You'll have to speak up, I've . . ."

One liver-spotted hand goes to the hearing aid plugged into his ear.

DeBoer reaches into his pocket, pulls out his badge

and holds it up. "Get out of the car, you old twat. Police emergency."

"Officer, what seems to be the—?"

"*Detective*," DeBoer says, finally losing his patience, snapping the badge wallet shut, shoving it back into his pocket and pulling open the car door. He grabs the old man by one shoulder and tries to drag him out but the man's seat belt is still buckled and holds him fast. DeBoer reaches in and punches the release switch then tries again. The old man tumbles free of the vehicle and falls to the wet road beneath.

"Officer, please," he protests, scrabbling for his glasses.

"Detective!" DeBoer shouts in his ear. "Fucking *detective,* you old coot!"

He steps over the man, straightens his raincoat, and gets into the car.

"Jesus Christ," DeBoer splutters, the steering wheel embedded in his gut and his knees jammed against the console. He fumbles for the seat's adjustment lever and attempts to slide the seat back to give himself more room but it's jammed tight, probably rusted in place after too many years in the same position.

The old man gets to his knees, sliding his glasses back onto his nose. One lens is badly cracked and an arm sticks out at an angle. "Officer—"

DeBoer slams the door shut. It's a struggle to manoeuvre his legs but at least it's an automatic so he only has to fight with the accelerator and not worry about a clutch as well. He sticks the car into gear, then leans out of the still-open window.

"It's *detective*!" DeBoer shouts one last time.

He hits the accelerator, leaving the old man stranded in the middle of the road and heading straight for the Wheatsheaf—and his way out of the hole he is currently occupying.

5.

Katja.

Not long after he arrives at the bar the name comes to him as he stands in a corner next to a concrete column, as far from the main crowd as possible, but still with a good view of the stage.

She no longer sports the large spikes of hair she had in the photo he had originally seen in the Policie report which had come from the island and in the vandalised poster for the gig, but despite that, and the large tattoo that covers her neck and some of her chest, he has no doubt it's her.

He watches her shriek and thrash about on stage, barking into the microphone as if she were an attack dog ravaging a coke dealer's arm, the neck of her guitar gripped in one hand, and can't help but feel contempt for everything and everyone around him. Sweaty, drunken, criminal fuckwits who think that making as much noise as possible is a valid substitute for melody. Those who are interested bounce around him like lunatics, almost colliding with him multiple times, but he resists the instinctive urge to grab them and punch the living shit out of them.

He refuses to let anything interfere with his reason for being there.

He bides his time, despite the agony of listening to the so-called music, beginning to wish he had taken the old man's hearing aid as well as his car. Maybe there would have been some sort of white noise setting to block the cacophony out.

Fortunately the soundcheck is as quick as sex with the prostitutes he frequented and so soon enough Katja pulls the guitar from her shoulder, revealing a skull spray-painted onto the T-shirt she wears.

"Yeah, fuck you, too," she says into the mic before she disappears.

DeBoer pushes through the crowd to keep her in sight, watches her vanish into the darkness of a corridor at the back of the stage. Thanks to a couple of busts he'd made on the place a year or so back, he knows where it leads and so hurriedly leaves. Scaffolding encrusts most of the front of the building and the scorch marks from the fire which had recently engulfed it remain like old scars, but everything is fine around the back.

He takes a dirty handkerchief from one pocket and then a small brown bottle from another. He removes a dropper from the bottle and places a few drops of liquid into the handkerchief then is about to head for the rear door to wait for her coming out when he hears footsteps.

He ducks into a doorway as four women walk past.

No. Wait.

He squints, his eyesight not what it used to be and his ears still ringing from the gig.

They aren't women at all.

Lady Delicious and her mob, he realizes.

He thinks of Frank's threat—his promise—to set the transvestite debt collector on him and decides to remain where he is. Ignoring his itching asshole, he watches the four confront Katja when she emerges from the Wheatsheaf and momentarily worries that he might miss his opportunity to cash in on her but in the end all they take from her is her guitar and perhaps a little self-respect. He leans farther back into the shadow of the doorway as they walk past him and a minute or so later Katja follows.

He lets her pass and turn onto the main thoroughfare then hurries to the car, parked up on the opposite side of the road to the Wheatsheaf and still with all its wheels intact. He squeezes himself back in, fumbling for the seat adjustment lever but finds it rusted into place, and so resigns himself to his discomfort. He watches Katja until she is a block or so away then starts the engine and pulls the vehicle onto the quiet streets. He drifts along as slowly as he dares, figuring that anyone seeing him will just assume him to be an old near-sighted coot, while always keeping Katja just in view and no more.

He almost loses her a couple of times as she makes her way through the streets via an unnecessarily complicated route, and wonders if perhaps she has spotted him after all. She slows as she approaches a row of buildings, once impressive three-storey homes now nothing more than brick and concrete bug shelters.

Without missing a beat, DeBoer stamps on the accelerator, having to wait several moments for the power to come through, then screeches to a halt metres away from her. He pulls himself from the car and she's running now, across a weed-choked lawn. He jumps at her, almost missing but coming down on her hard enough to crash her to the ground beneath him. He pulls her hood away, revealing her closely shaven scalp. She manages to slam an elbow into his face before he snatches the handkerchief, freshly soaked in chloroform, and shoves it into her face. She throws her head from side to side but already the chemical is taking effect and her movements become sluggish. He loosens his grip on her and lets her turn herself onto her back. He fingers his cheekbone where she had struck him but the damage is minimal.

Katja looks up at him, her lids heavy, squinting against the light of a street lamp behind him. She says something but her words are slurred.

He leans into her, pressing the handkerchief to her face once more. "Stop fucking *fighting*, you little tramp."

She claws at his hands but her fingers are limp and ineffective. Within moments her limbs slump to the ground beside her.

"I know who you are, Katja," he says, unable to control his joy at having caught her. "And I think we both know that there are certain people who would just love to get their hands on you."

He wants her to see him. He wants her to know what lies in store for her, to suffer that knowledge.

She murmurs slurred words and he turns his head to one side to hear her better. "I'm sorry, you'll have to speak up. I'm deaf as a tent-pole from that fucking racket you were playing."

"Useless. Fucking. Junkie," she says and then her eyes roll back in her head and she is gone.

6.

Seven of them in total, in the middle of the vacant parking lot of a burger joint which is no longer there, all lined up like school kids after a fire alarm.

A woman with bright pink, dyed hair clipped in place with a dozen little clasps stands before them. She holds a clipboard in purple-gloved hands and one by one takes down the details of those gathered.

Nikolai recognises most of them as scene regulars—a collection of chemical misfits and wasters who are probably as close as he will come to a social circle. As he waits for his turn, he studies the crumpled leaflet he holds in one hand, the same leaflet some of the others have brought with them, torn from the walls of research labs and universities and subtly noting the details for the gathering. In his other hand, something that none of the others have—a poster for a punk gig.

The Broken, a dense, jagged scrawl announces, along with the dates and times of the show.

And a picture of a girl, one hand clutching a microphone

so tightly the bones of her hand show through the graininess of the printing.

Despite the shaven head and new tattoos he has no doubt that it is Katja. He recognised her the moment he came across the poster earlier that day, the first time he had seen her face since being kicked out of the Stumps a couple of months earlier. After he had fucked up yet again.

"Not seen you around for a while," one of the others says to him as they wait. "I heard you got into a lock-away?"

The man who stands beside Nikolai is short and weedy looking with lank hair tied back in a ponytail. He's wearing a death metal band T-shirt and his smile is punctuated by only three or four crooked, stained teeth. He wears a small chain with his name spelled out in little silver letters: DAMIEN.

Nikolai shrugs. "It was a . . . a laxative."

"And did it work?"

"You said yourself you've not seen me around for a couple of weeks—what do you think?"

"Eeep," Damien says.

The woman with the pink hair and clipboard moves onto the next volunteer.

Damien nudges Nikolai. "Thought I'd landed myself a dream one a week or so back."

Nikolai ignores him but the man continues. "Some sort of sex pill. They had this other pill that was like an off-switch for it but they'd been having problems getting it to function in their previous test subjects so I basically spent a solid week fucking day and night whilst they figured out what was causing it to not function. One hundred bucks and a bunch of weeping sores, that's all I got out of it. Wouldn't have been so bad if the women they'd brought in had been something to look at, I'm telling you."

Nikolai continues ignoring him.

"One hundred fucking bucks, how can they expect us to live on that? I spent the lot on creams for the sores which they didn't even provide as part of the trial, by the way, those cheap bastards. This one, on the other hand— it's that old inverse proportion rule, right?"

"The what?"

"You know. The shittier the location we have to go to for assessment, the more underground it all is, the better the pay. And vice versa."

He stops talking when the woman with the clipboard reaches him.

She shines a small torch into his eyes, examining his pupil response, then asks him to open his mouth and shines it in there too. Her lip curls involuntarily at the sight of his crooked teeth. She asks him several questions, then scribbles down his responses on her notepad.

"Are you currently on any medication?"

"Nope," Damien says, winks at Nikolai.

"Any illegal substances?" she asks, as aware as those gathered that it's like asking a prisoner if they are innocent.

"No ma'am," he says and winks again.

The woman makes more notes then takes a step back and looks him up and down. She says, "Thank you."

She repeats the procedure with Nikolai, checking his eyes and mouth, then his fingernails.

"Are you currently on any medication?"

"No."

He's aware of Damien grinning madly beside him but takes no notice.

"Any illegal substances?"

"I'm clean," Nikolai answers.

"Thank you," she says, then turns and flicks through her sheets of notes. She walks up the line and back again and it shifts with her presence as if she exerts some sort of gravitational pull on each person there.

"You," she says finally, pointing her pen at Nikolai.

He hesitates then steps forward when she motions for him to come towards her. He stands beside her, looking back at the crowd from which he has been plucked.

"Thank you all for coming," she says and then guides Nikolai towards the cherry red Honda she had arrived in.

"You're fucking kidding me. That's it?!" one of the others complains, loudly enough for the woman to hear. "You're only taking *one*?"

"One is all we're looking for, guys," she says, opening the door for Nikolai. He climbs inside.

"And you choose *him*?" Damien shouts. "He's the biggest fucking junkie out of all of us!"

She closes Nikolai's door and climbs into the driver's seat. "Maybe next time fellas," she says.

The group has now gathered in front of the car, blocking its exit. The woman starts the engine, revs it a couple of times. She hits the headlights, flooding the group in light and for a few moments there is a stand-off, nobody prepared to make the first move. Finally the crowd splits, though only just enough for her to squeeze the car through them, and, as she passes, fists and palms slap against the roof and window.

She pulls the car onto the main road and joins the light traffic, glances in her rearview mirror at Nikolai.

"It's not true," he tells her, nervously rubbing his hands across his thighs. "I'm not . . . taking anything. Not anymore."

The woman says nothing, her indifference as tangible as it had been when assessing them. She swings the car into a u-turn to head back the way she came.

Nikolai looks out the window as they pass the parking lot.

Damien stands at the front of the crowd and gives him the finger.

"I hope they *fuck you up, Nikolai*!" he shouts, then disappears from sight.

But before that, there was this. . . .

• • •

Bridget watches the couple from a booth at the back of the club, away from the main throng and bathed in the glow from a couple of slot machines lined up against one wall.

The woman is of medium height with rich black hair, multiple tattoos adorning her arms. The man is taller, bright blue eyes and short blonde hair. He says something and the woman laughs, placing a hand on his chest, fingers spread.

Bridget sips at a glass of water, leaning to one side when someone entering blocks her view momentarily.

"Loving your look," another man says to her. He wears a suit with his tie and top shirt buttons loosened, the gel in his hair losing a battle to keep it slicked back from his forehead.

She follows his gaze to her hands, sheathed in purple latex gloves. She tucks them into her pockets, removing them from sight.

"How do you get your hair that colour? So pink?"

"I dye it."

"Oh. May I?" the man asks, already starting to sit down.

Bridget blocks him with one booted foot, shakes her head. "Sorry," she says, then peers over his shoulder.

The couple are leaning into one another, exchanging breath and scents. The woman stands and pulls her coat on. The two make their way through the crowd.

Bridget gets up, pushes past the man without another word, and hurries to follow the couple outside.

A cold breeze snaps her to attention as she looks farther up the street. Locked in one another's arms, the couple stagger along then cross the road before entering an apartment block. She climbs three floors and unlocks the door to her apartment, snaps on a light. On the wall beside her is a large corkboard littered with photographs of the man she had been watching in the club; some of them blurry Polaroids, others what look like grainy screen-grabs. Amongst these are sticky notes with times and addresses scribbled on them.

She peels off her gloves and takes a fresh set from a box on the counter, pulls them on.

She crosses to a desk on top of which are several small

TVs and powers them on one by one. Static slowly gives way.

The first is a row of apartment blocks similar to Bridget's own, fronted by a communal grassy court. The scene emerges just as the couple she had been watching come into view. They walk across the grass, the man's hand sliding up and down the woman's arm, caressing her tattoos, then they enter one of the buildings.

Bridget's attention switches to the next screen, awkwardly positioned on top of two VCR decks. This one is a stairwell, the lighting dim but the couple still recognisable at the edge of the picture. The man presses the woman against a wall, kissing her neck. The woman smiles, then eases him away, takes his hand and leads up towards the stairs.

The next screen, showing a small and cluttered studio apartment. There's a flare of light as a door opens, the glare blinding Bridget's view like a nuclear blast. When it subsides the couple are wrapped in one another's arms, frantically removing each other's clothing. The door slams shut behind them. They move out of view.

The next screen is blank. Bridget waits, thinking it is just too dark to see anything, then slaps the side of the device. The TV blinks into life, the image jumping and fizzing. She hits it again and a bed comes into focus.

The woman lies out on it, her arms extended above her head towards the pillows as the man tugs at her jeans to remove them.

Bridget opens a drawer in a unit next to the TVs and removes a headset of the sort call centre workers would wear. The audio cable ends in a small, plastic box. She slides a button to switch it on and a red light glows. In her ears now, the sounds of laboured breathing. She closes her eyes to it for a few moments then opens them again. Reaches in with her gloved hands and removes a small, latex-coated vibrator.

She pulls a small armchair into position before the TVs and settles into it.

The couple are both down to their underwear now, the woman almost lost beneath the broad expanse of the man's back. Her legs wrap around the back of his.

Bridget lifts her skirt and switches the vibrator on.

7.

She watches the man pull on his trousers and T-shirt then quickly tie his shoelaces.

He says something to the woman but the words are lost amidst static crackle. Bridget takes off the headphones and lets them sit around her neck. Then the man is gone from the TV screen, appearing on the one showing the staircase a minute or so later, still tucking himself in. Back on the bedroom camera the woman is now getting dressed, buttoning her jeans and pulling on a fresh T-shirt, black with the yellow smiley face on it, her tattoos like bruises in amongst the graininess. She quickly re-applies some make-up then pulls on a jacket and leaves the apartment.

With the woman gone, Bridget gets up and cracks open a fresh bottle of whiskey. She tips a couple of fingers into a glass then adds some coke. Swallows half of it in one go. Tops up the liquor.

She quickly burns through two glasses and is pouring herself a third when there is a knock at the door. She checks the spyhole before undoing the locks.

"Hey Liz," she says, opening the door and letting her visitor in.

The woman breezes past Bridget, removes her coat and hangs it up on a peg on the back of the door. Medium height with rich black hair and multiple tattoos peeking out from beneath a black T-shirt emblazoned with a yellow smiley face.

"Thanks," Liz says, taking the whiskey and coke from Bridget and downing several large gulps before handing it back to her. "You mind if I—?"

She doesn't wait for an answer, crossing to the counter and pouring a glass for herself. She takes a swig, brushes her hair from her face.

"Well?"

"Well what?" Liz asks.

"How . . . how was it?"

Liz smiles, takes another swig. "How did it look?"

"Fine," she says. "Good, I mean."

"Yeah, well, that's because you didn't smell him," Liz counters.

"Smell him?"

"Stank like he hadn't taken a shower in a week."

"Oh," Bridget says, taking a sip of her own drink. "I thought he looked nice."

"He looked the part, I'll give you that. But not everything comes across through the screens, Bridget, you know?"

"Yeah."

"He screwed pretty good but we're not having him again, okay?"

"Okay," Bridget says, knowing she has little choice

in the matter despite all the planning she put into the evening.

Liz returns the armchair to its normal position in front of a larger TV suspended from the adjacent wall, then sits down. Bridget turns off the little screens one by one, then the recording decks beneath them. She plucks the photos and sticky notes from the corkboard and drops them into a wire-rimmed bin.

"Then we'll find someone else," she says, stamping on them to crush them into the bin. "Tonight."

"*Tonight?*"

"Hey, you may have gotten your rocks off but I certainly haven't," she says. "And this time *I* get to choose, okay?"

"Okay," Bridget says.

Liz grabs a pen and paper from the desk next to the TVs and scrawls the word *Romeo* across the top of the first page.

"First up—looks," she says. "Johnny Cash—obviously. A young one . . ."

She writes that down then tilts her head upwards in thought. "What else?" she ponders aloud, rolling the pen around in her mouth, the devious grin still on her lips. "Smart. He's got to be, like, stupid smart."

"Body?"

"Athletic is fine. Oh and maybe a bit of nail polish or eyeliner just to spice things up."

"You don't ask for much do you?" Bridget says, downing the rest of her drink and perching on the side of the chair. "Look, I've got to head out for a bit,"

"Now?"

"Yeah."

"But what about my dream man?"

"I won't be long, I promise."

"At this time of night, what . . . ?" Her words trail and she feels stupid for even having asked the question. "Oh."

"I'll be as quick as I can," Bridget says, taking a clipboard and pen from another drawer in the desk.

"I'll be waiting," Liz sings, adjusting her position to get comfy in the chair. Then, more seriously, "Be careful, okay?"

Bridget says goodbye then is gone. Liz shifts her position again, something hard beneath her, then reaches under her legs.

Pulls out the vibrator.

8.

Leaving the line of wasters standing in the rain, Bridget drives across town then turns the car into the small private parking lot at the front of Stasko's clinic, stopping next to the surgeon's racing-green sports car.

She gets out then opens the door for her passenger, motioning for him to get out. He does as instructed, looking up at the brief line of business shop-fronts to either side of the clinic. She knows he'll be wondering why the clinic is open so late but says nothing as she leads him up to the front door.

Inside, the building is compact and head-ache white, each surface gleaming and sparkling. The main corridor is short and empty save for a framed painting, Roland Penrose's *Octavia*, and a small shelf on which a high-heeled boot is placed. They follow the corridor into a reception and waiting area with elegantly designed Swedish furniture and a small collection of high-end fashion magazines scattered across a glass table. A young woman is seated in one of the high-backed, white metal chairs, her manicured hands clasped over a large leather-bound book. She looks up at Bridget as they pass and there is a moment of recognition there but Bridget leads the guinea pig past her and through another door.

Beyond the door the lights are out, save for the glow coming from one room at the end of another short corridor. Bridget leads the man to one of the smaller operating theatres and snaps the lights on. They buzz overhead for several moments, flicker and flash, then illuminate the room. Again everywhere is a pure white—one wall lined with shining cupboards and a chair of the sort a dentist might use in the middle of the room.

"Take a seat," Bridget tells the man. He looks momentarily panicked until she points to the small stool next to the operating chair. "If you could fill this form in and give me a sample of your urine—there's a small toilet in the corner there if you want to use it. I'll be back in a minute to collect some blood."

He nods, still assessing the room and possibly the situation he has allowed himself to be led into, and Bridget leaves, heading for the room at the end of the corridor. She knocks gently then opens the door.

Stasko is bent over the architect-style drawing table before her, furiously scribbling some measurements into a small notepad.

"Bridget," he says without looking up.

"He's in the other room," Bridget says, remaining in the doorway.

Stasko turns, flipping up the magnifying glass which is clipped to his glasses. "Of course," he says, smiling vaguely. "You got one?"

She nods. "He's filling out an assessment form. Who's the girl?"

"What girl?"

"The girl in the waiting room."

He considers this. "Oh," he says finally. "She's still there? Of course she is."

"Isn't that what the . . ."

She indicates the sketches and measurements pinned to the drawing table.

"Yes. Yes. That's correct."

"Are you okay, Doctor? You seem a little distracted."

He nods but it doesn't seem to be in response to her question, instead the response to some internal dialogue she is not privy to.

"I have something else I need you to do for me, Bridget."

"What do you mean?"

He rubs his jaw and stands and she can see a mad sparkle in his eyes. He holds up one of the pieces of paper magnetically pinned to the drawing board. It appears to a poster of some sort, badly photocopied and with hand-scrawled print on it instead of proper lettering. The bottom half has been torn away but the top half reveals a demented, screaming woman with spiked hair and something jutting from her neck.

"Did you make that?" she asks him, wondering if his grief was finally starting to spiral fully out of control.

He shakes his head, the nervous energy within him palpable as he hands the poster to her. "I want you to find her, Bridget. I want you to bring her to me."

"Bring who to you?" Bridget asks.

"*Her*," Stasko says, stabbing a finger at the poster.

"Doctor, I thought I'd already made it clear I don't want to get involved in . . . that side of things."

"You brought me the guinea pig."

"And that's as far as it goes. I've just brought him to you—what you do with him is between you and him."

"Nurse Soelberg," he says, leaning in closer. She knows the switch to the more formal method of addressing her is deliberate, that it is designed to reminds her of his authority over her. "We spend all day plumping people's lips, paralysing them with toxins and sucking out pieces of them through a hose only to pump it back in somewhere else. People have domain over their own bodies so that they can choose to do whatever they like to them. There's no difference between what goes on here during the day—and what goes on at night."

"The difference is I only work during the day."

"You work when I need you to work," he says, his voice still calm but his teeth clenched. "All I'm asking is that you find this girl and bring her to me just like you brought me the guinea pig. Bring her to me and your involvement will end there, I assure you, Bridget."

Back to her first name again.

"How am I meant to find her?"

She looks down at the poster. Whatever details there had been as to what the poster had been for must have been on the part that has been torn off.

"You're a bright girl," he tells her. "As soon as I have finished with my patient I'll participate in the search but for now I must delegate to my most trusted employee. I'm sure you'll figure something out."

He removes the woollen sweater vest he wears and plucks his doctor's whites from a hook on the wall.

"What about the guinea pig?" she asks.

"Have you finished his assessment yet?"

Shakes her head. "I still have to run bloods and urine."

"Good, then get it done now before you leave and have him sent to me afterwards. Walk with me."

He holds the door open for her, making it clear that she has no choice but to accompany him.

They stop by the door to the surgery and Stasko puts a hand on her shoulder. "I trust you will achieve," he says, then strides down to the waiting area.

A few moments later he emerges with the woman from the waiting room and now Bridget gets a clearer view of her she realizes how young she is—probably no more than eighteen. Her lips are painted purple and sparkle with a pair of lip rings and there is a hesitancy to her movements as she is led out the front door of the clinic by Stasko. She looks over her shoulder, exchanging the briefest of glances with Bridget, before the door closes.

Bridget enters the surgery to find the guinea pig still seated where she had left him, the form she gave him now filled with his personal details. She scans it quickly.

"It's all I could manage," he says, holding up the plastic sample bottle filled with a small amount of a dark orange liquid. "Sorry, I must be kind of . . . dehydrated."

"It's fine," she says, then checks the name he has noted down. "Nikolai."

She takes the bottle from him and inserts it into a little pocket attached to the assessment form.

"I wouldn't have thought that was your type of music," he says.

"I'm sorry?"

Then she realizes he is looking at the poster Stasko had given her, still clasped in one hand. "Your gig poster."

She shrugs. "Is it your type?" she asks absently as she completes some of the details on his form.

"Used to be," Nikolai says. Then he adds, "I know her."

"Know who?" Bridget asks, not really paying attention, just wanting to get it all over and done with and back to Liz.

"The girl in the poster. Katja."

Bridget stops writing and looks up. "Know her how?" she asks suspiciously.

"I . . . I used to be in a band with her. We stayed in the same squat. But then . . ."

"You stay in the same squat?"

"Used to," Nikolai corrects her.

"But you know where she lives?"

Nikolai suddenly becomes defensive, perhaps sensing the urgency in her voice. "Well, I mean, I could be wrong, it sort of looks like her but then . . ."

"It's okay, I'm a fan," Bridget reassures him. "I mean, I've heard that she's worth seeing, that the band is worth seeing. Is this a gig poster, is that what it is? I found it but it was all torn."

"I don't know," Nikolai says, nervous twitches starting to affect him. "It could be, I don't know anything about it."

"Come on, Nikolai, I just want the chance to meet her. I . . . I want to form my own band, you know? This job only just pays the bills. If I could just talk to her, get some tips. I could maybe swing an increase in your fee?"

He stops rubbing his legs but doesn't look up. Several seconds of silence pass, then:

"Yeah I know where she lives," he says.

9.

Bridget has been in the car long enough for her breath to start fogging the windscreen when she spots someone walking towards the building she's been watching. Small and wearing a hooded top, arms wrapped around themselves, it's difficult to tell age or whether the figure is male or female but it's the only person she has seen in a long while.

She sits bolt upright as headlights flash across her rear view mirror, quickly followed by the screech of tires. She looks out the window in time to see an old station wagon ramp up onto the curb outside the building and a man pull himself free of the vehicle. He stumbles out of it and chases after the hooded figure, jumping on his target and sending them both crashing to the ground. Bridget continues to watch the two struggle, resisting the urge to start the engine and get out of there, but if the guinea pig were to tell Stasko about the information he had given her then the surgeon would be expecting something as a result.

The man, fat and swathed in a dirty raincoat,

presses himself down onto the hooded figure, clutching something to his prey's face.

"Come on, Bridget, *do* something," she says to herself, taking out the hypodermic syringe she had prepared earlier. She opens the car door, the screams coming from across the road now clearly female. The man lifts the woman's prone form onto his shoulders and carries her back to his car.

"Wait. Just wait," Bridget mutters. Her hands, now in a fresh pair of purple latex gloves, are shaking. "I don't even know if it's her."

The man opens the rear door of his car and shoves the body inside, dusts off his hands. Places a handkerchief back in his pocket.

When he's circling around to the front of the car Bridget finally jumps out, keeping her head low as she crosses to him.

He hears the sound of her footfall but only at the last moment. By that time the needle is already sunk deep into the flabby tissue at the back of his neck and the effect is almost instantaneous. His body first goes rigid, hands coming up to his neck but not quite making it before everything goes limp and he crashes to the ground like a felled walrus. Bridget watches over him until she is certain that he is out cold then reaches into his coat pocket and takes out his wallet. She pulls out some old, stained business cards. A fucking detective.

"Shit," she says, suddenly panicking that there will be others, wondering if she has just interrupted some sort of police operation but when nothing happens she hurriedly opens the rear of the car.

The woman's hood has been pulled off and Bridget takes the gig poster from her pocket and unfolds it, matching the two despite the murky light and the fact that the woman's head was clean-shaven rather than littered with spikes. Bridget leans in closer, checks the woman is still breathing then examining the extensive tattoo which covers her neck, running a gloved finger across it. She feels something embedded in the skin beneath the design and instantly knows that it is the reason that Stasko is after her.

She reaches in and, with some difficulty, manages to haul the body up onto her shoulder. She staggers across the road and cracks open the rear door to her own vehicle, shoves the woman inside. Slams the door shut, starts the engine.

The car tires squeal as they try to find purchase and as she drives off she glances in the rear view mirror at the still-prone figure of the fat man, wondering what the hell kind of trouble Katja is already involved in.

10.

Flesh Heel is busy with the usual clientele when Bridget enters. Loud darkwave music blasts from speakers positioned around the club, deftly controlled by a man in an expensive-looking metal and latex outfit lurking behind a set of decks in one corner. Neon tube lights of varying colour adorn the walls along with metallic whips and casts of various body parts, curtains of chain-mail, and paintings of latex-clad women. More latex-clad women sit in the booths beneath them as if they have just stepped out of the portraits, nursing vibrant cocktails and pitchers of dark purple liquid.

Bridget adjusts her grip on Katja, the other woman's arm hooked around her shoulder and gripped by the wrist. A few look up as they pass but merely give Bridget a knowing look, perhaps having been in a similar situation themselves or hoping to achieve it by the end of the night. She manages to haul Katja through the club and to a door at the back of the bar area.

She punches a code into the security keypad mounted

on the door frame. There's an electronic click as the lock is released. She struggles to get the door open while maintaining her grip on Katja, only just managing to get through without letting the unconscious woman tumble to the floor. The door seals shut behind them on weighted hinges and instantly the atmosphere changes.

Silence swapped for the pounding industrial throb of the music.

A cool, almost clinical air, swapped for the sweaty heat of the club.

She descends a mercifully short set of steps into the basement and calls out Stasko's name.

The room which extends beyond the stairs is kitted out with exactly the same gleaming white fittings as the clinic, lit by an enormous surgical lamp which looms over a gurney like a predator. The girl from the clinic lies on the table, limbs slightly parted, her hair wrapped in disposable plastic. A green sheet is spread across her and there's a bloody gauze taped over her mouth out of which a small piece of tubing emerges. Another breath-restriction fetishist, Bridget realizes. Her breathing is steady and calm, a couple of machines to one side monitoring her sedation.

Stasko is in the far corner, bent over a sink and scrubbing blood and iodine from his hands. He knocks the tap with one elbow when he becomes aware of Bridget's presence. His face lights up when he realizes she is not alone and he rushes to them.

"You found her already? *How?*"

Bridget hands Katja's limp form over to him, deciding not to mention the information Nikolai had given her.

She might as well get the credit if she can get away with it.

"Does it matter?"

Stasko holds Katja around the waist as if he is clutching his lover after a fainting episode. He gently runs his hand across her face and scalp then over her neck. He feels what Bridget had earlier felt, the little protrusion from the middle of her neck, almost lost amidst the tattoo. He uses his pinkie to prod it and lets out a sigh.

"So we're done?" Bridget asks, already stepping back towards the stairs.

Stasko barely acknowledges her, nodding absently but still studying Katja intently.

"Get her cleaned up and into the recovery suite," he says, vaguely indicating the girl on the operating table.

"Are you sure she's ready to . . ."

"Now, Nurse Soelberg," Stasko insists.

"Yes doctor."

11.

Katja emerges back into consciousness like a bead of blood into new tattoo.

Each time the room around her comes into focus it quickly shivers and fades again, dragging her even deeper back into the haze which had previously consumed her. Her limbs feel heavy and a crashing headache throbs within her skull. She tries to move but can't. She hears footsteps and an occasional electronic beep. She becomes aware of someone in the room beside her.

She does her best to focus her every thought on breaking free of the darkness and finally it peels away from her. Bright light rushes in, causing little spikes of pain to shoot through her eyeballs. Her throat feels raw, each swallow like knocking back a shot of broken glass, and when she tries to touch it she finds that her hands won't move.

She looks down, blinking to clear the remainder of the drug-fog, and realizes that she is lying on a hospital gurney, her wrists and ankles held in place by black leather restraints.

"What . . . the hell . . . ?"

A figure appears next to her, almost entirely described in silhouette but she just barely makes out the surgical scrubs and mask.

"Am I . . . in hospital?"

"No," the man says. "Why, are you ill?"

"I . . ."

Katja tries once more to sit up but the restraints hold tight. She blinks some more and the initial dazzle of the light fades away as her eyes adjust. She struggles to recall how she got here, remembers the gig. No—the sound check. Then after that?

Heels. Why is she thinking about high heels? And a fat man, reeking of an ugly body odour. A chemical burning at her nostrils. These pieces float around her, refusing to settle into any sensible order.

I know who you are, Katja. And I think we both know that there are certain people who would just love to get their hands on you.

X-rays and sketches are pinned to the wall above her, enlarged photos of what she instantly recognises to be her own neck.

The surgeon leans over her, his gloved hands working their way across her chest and throat.

"Healing well," he says. "I do not understand why you would have wanted to cut the tube out in the first place. Such a shame. But this one is much improved anyway."

He holds a small mirror up, presenting her with the image of a gleaming new tracheotomy tube protruding from the midst of the tattoo which she had gotten to cover up the remainder of her previous one.

"What the . . . fuck is . . . this?"

"Beautiful," the surgeon says, too focused on her neck to properly hear the question. "A good start."

"Start of what?"

He puts the mirror to one side, regarding her with puzzlement, as if he couldn't contemplate why she would ask such a thing. "Your transformation."

And he waves a hand across the collection of prints and x-rays pinned to the wall.

Katja examines them more carefully, realising that there are Polaroids of people in amongst the sketches, people with strange additions and modifications to their heads and bodies. They're still bloody from whatever operations they have been through, still marked with dotted incision lines.

"You're fuck . . . ing . . . kidding . . . meee," she slurs.

"You have nothing to worry about," he tells her. "What Anna and I had planned for . . . you are so much like her. So much like her in so many ways."

He removes his gloves, runs a hand across Katja's shaven scalp. She wriggles beneath him but her body is still refusing to fully co-operate.

"But this is enough for one night. You need to keep your strength up."

He goes around the back of the gurney, out of her line of sight, then pushes her across the makeshift surgery towards a door at the rear.

"I am going to unstrap you now, Katja. I should warn you that if you try anything I have a dose of sedative here. I haven't properly calculated the dosage based on your body weight so whilst it might not be lethal, I cannot guarantee it. I would hate to lose you so early on and I'm sure you will be keen to not lose yourself either, yes?"

He holds up a syringe to prove his point. She nods and so he undoes her straps one by the one, watching her the whole time.

"There," he says when done. "Can you stand for me?"

He slides an arm underneath her back and assists her into a sitting position, then onto her feet. She grits her teeth, fighting for control of her own limbs, her legs threatening to give way beneath her. She scans the room whilst the surgeon punches a code into a keypad mounted on the wall, calculating any potential escape routes, but the staircase behind him appears to be the only way out and she has no idea what it leads to. The surgeon opens the door, the room beyond is no more than twelve feet by twelve feet and swathed in darkness. A bed lies up against the far corner, a chrome wash basin in one of the others. The surgeon helps her to the bed, lays her down.

"Get some rest," he tells her, smiling. "I will be back soon and we can begin the next procedure."

"So who is it then?" she asks him, still wary of the syringe he holds. "One of Szerynski's lot? It can't be Kohl—that one couldn't organise a fuck in a brothel."

"I have no idea what you are talking about," he says. "Please, get some rest."

He closes the door and the sound of his footsteps quickly fades.

Katja forces herself upright, one arm on the wall beside her. Her eyes now fight to re-adjust, the stark illumination of the surgery swapped once more for darkness.

She staggers across the room and tries the door handle but it holds fast. She bangs on the door, snarling threats into it, all the while feeling as if she is about to collapse. She feels her way around the room blindly, checking for taped-up windows or ventilation shafts, anything. She finds a light switch and hits it, a strip-light buzzing into weak life above her.

And then someone says, "Katja?"

She freezes, finger still on the switch, recognising the voice instantly.

12.

After having had his blood drawn Nikolai is led out of the clinic by the nurse with the pink hair.

She locks up and he gets back into her car. She drives him a short distance to a club district and into a building with the words *Flesh Heel* emblazoned across the front doors in reflective paint. A queue of people in fetishwear line up behind a rope guarded by doormen so beefed up it appears as if their shoulders have enveloped their necks. They step to one side when they see the nurse and open the doors for her. Nikolai is quickly guided through the smoke- and neon-filled room, past people gyrating and wrapped around one another, past the bar lit from beneath in a cold blue light, and into a rear passageway.

"Where are we going?" he asks her.

She doesn't answer, leads him down a set of steps and into a makeshift surgery.

A girl lies out on an operating table and Nikolai recognises her as the one from clinic. Her head is turned to one side and she is staring right at him but her eyes are glassy, vacant. A man dressed in surgical smocks, including a facial mask and cap, looks up from the instrument tray he is arranging. He nods at the woman and she takes Nikolai's arm, guides him to a door at the back of the room and enters a secure code, and then they go inside.

She flicks a light switch on, revealing a small, sparse room with a basic wire-framed bed on either side and a chrome washbasin in between.

"Get some rest," she tells him.

The sound of a drill revving up echoes through from the surgery beyond.

"I thought this was just going to be some tests," he says as he is sat down on the bed. "I mean . . ."

The whirring increases in intensity and volume from outside, matching the speed of Nikolai's hands rubbing up and down his legs.

"Don't worry about that," she tells him. "It's unrelated."

"Oh. Good."

"I'm going to turn the light off so you can get some rest, okay?"

Before he can say anything the room is plunged into darkness as the door closes, muffling the noises coming from the surgery beyond.

"Shit," he mutters.

Without knowing what else to do he settles down on the bed, remaining in the darkness for what seems like hours until the door opens once more and a woman is brought in by the surgeon. Nikolai can only make out the vaguest impressions of them but even in the low light he thinks he recognises her.

The surgeon closes the door and she launches herself at it, slamming her fists against it and screaming obscenities then scrabbling around the room, her hands just barely brushing him at one point, until she finds the light switch. She hits it and now he is certain.

"Katja," he says.

And perhaps being locked in the room with the surgeon might not be the worst possibility after all.

"*Nikolai?*" she says, turning around. "You're fucking kidding me."

"I didn't think I . . . what are you doing here?"

"You first."

"Another medical study. I think."

She looks at him for a few moments, taking in the fresh plasters rimmed with dried blood on the back of his hands and inner arm.

"You're here for the trial too?"

"Tell me, Nikolai," she says with menace, ignoring his question. "Does the name Lady Delicious ring any bells?"

"Lady who?"

"Ah, I see," she says, arms crossed as she walks towards him. He backs farther into the corner. "So you don't remember taking out a loan in the name of the band?"

"A *loan?*"

"Yes, a fucking *loan!*" she screams. "A fucking *loan* which that demented bitch and her gang of tranny psychos are now expecting *me* to settle! I hope it was money well spent, Nikolai, I hope you got utterly off your face on it."

Nikolai says nothing.

"I *trusted* you, Nik. I stood up for you! I told the rest of the band you were clean and then what do you go and do? You turn up to rehearsals whacked out of your little mind."

And it's as if the last couple of months haven't happened, their current argument seamlessly entwining with the one they had had the last time they were together.

"Well, I've got news for you," she continues. "The band is doing just fucking fine without you. Joey stepped in."

"Oh," he says. Then, "I saw your poster. The gig."

And he takes the folded up scrap of paper from his back pocket, unravels it and shows it to her.

"Yeah, well it ain't going to happen if I'm locked up here much longer," she says quietly. She looks around the room, examining it in more detail now that it is lit.

She climbs up on the other bed, running her hands along the wall as if hoping to find a secret lever or door.

"Katja," he says eventually. "I'm sorry."

He's lost track of the number of times he's apologised to her after what happened but each time the sentiment has less and less meaning—though what else can he do?

And then he realizes exactly what he can do.

13.

DeBoer rolls the syringe back and forth between his palms, the remaining trickle of liquid glinting in the moonlight coming in through the station wagon's windshield. He rubs at the back of his neck to work away the lingering numbness, winces when he touches the little lump where the needle was shoved into him.

He was still woozy from the injection when he threw his weight around inside the squat, threatening whomever he found, demanding that they tell him where Katja was, but it had gotten him nowhere. So here he is now, back in the crappy old-man car, parked outside a welding plant, a shift just ending and the workers, their overalls filthy and their hair matted with sweat, emerging onto the street.

DeBoer licks his fingers, straightens his moustache, then gets out.

His legs are more stable now, willing to go along with the request to stride towards the workers. His raincoat billows around him and the men spot him when he is still several metres away but he is honing in on one in particular. His target sees him coming and there's a moment where it looks like the man is going to run before thinking better of it and coming to a halt. The other workers keep moving, isolating him.

"Well, well, look at you, McAuley," DeBoer says.

The man is almost entirely constructed of bones and skin with no underlying tissue, everything sharp angles and stretched white. He's stripped his overalls to the waist and they lie folded back there and tied in a knot like flayed skin. The shock of white hair on his head is smeared with grease.

"What's this, you've finally gone all respectable on me?"

McAuley shrugs. "I have a kid now."

DeBoer snorts. "Dragged from the shallow end of the gene pool just like Daddy I'm guessing. And don't tell me you spawned it with that whore you were with last time I saw you?"

Anger flares in McAuley but he holds it back. "I'm just trying to do what's right by them, Detective. Getting things straightened out. What do you want?"

"Don't get uppity with me you piece of shit," DeBoer snaps, stepping up to McAuley and shoving the man's head into the brick wall behind him. "I can drag you down to the interrogation room if you prefer? Huh? You want me to haul you down there?"

McAuley shakes his head, rubbing the back of it and avoiding eye contact.

"Good." DeBoer reaches into his coat and pulls out one of the posters of Katja which he had torn from a wall, holds it up.

"You know her?"

"No."

"I want to find her, you hear me?"

"B-but it says right there she'll be at the Wheatsheaf tonight."

"I fucking know that!" DeBoer snaps. "But I don't want to have to wait that long! Spread the word through this shitting city, I want everyone to know I'm looking for her. I'm about to put a cat amongst the chickens, you hear me? Go tell all your little rat-bastard friends."

"Detective, I'm not hanging with that lot any more, I already told you. I'm going straight."

DeBoer laughs. "Where have I heard that one before?"

"I've got a job, I'm taking care of my family."

"*I don't give a fuck about your fucking family, McAuley!*" DeBoer shouts and slams the man's head back against the wall again. "You think you're going straight then just fucking *unstraighten* yourself, you hear me? Get back into the gutters you came from and find out where this girl is or so help me god I'll make sure you have no *reason* to go straight. *Do you understand me?*"

"Detective, I—"

Another shove of the head and this time McAuley staggers and almost falls over, only just steadying himself against the wall. DeBoer can see the anger in the man's eyes, the frustration and sadness, and it makes the detective grin broadly.

"People like you *don't go straight*, McAuley," DeBoer says, brushing at his coat. Then over his shoulder as he walks back to the car, "I'll be expecting to hear from you shortly."

14.

Nikolai crosses to the washbasin, while Katja continues to check for a way out.

He squirts liquid soap from a dispenser mounted on the wall above the sink into his hand, sniffs it. Licks it. Grimaces. It tastes like a hospital smells. He ducks down and squirts more of the stuff into his mouth and swishes it around.

"What the hell are you doing?" Katja asks, staring at him with disgust.

"I can get us out of here," he says, the words distorted by the pinkish mess dribbling down his chin.

"By eating soap?"

He holds up a hand to tell her to wait. She crosses her arms impatiently.

"Well?"

And then he punches her.

The blow sends her spinning sideways. She stumbles towards the wall, steadies herself, then looks up, blinking and holding the side of her head. Her skin is flushed at the impact point, the promise of a nice dark bruise to follow.

"What the fuck did you—"

He grabs her, shoves her into the small room's only door. Katja grunts and pushes back and they struggle for a few moments before she breaks away. Nikolai trips her and she crashes to the ground, slamming her head off of it.

Then there's the sound of the door's locking mechanism disengaging. Nikolai backs away as the surgeon enters.

"What in the name of god is . . . ?"

His words fade. Katja on the floor, the side of her head red and slightly puffy, dazed looking. Nikolai standing over her, eyes bloodshot, frothing at the mouth.

The surgeon goes to Katja, wary of the insane druggie sharing the room with them but far more concerned with checking that she is okay, and as he reaches for Katja she lashes out, her boot slamming into his neck and knocking him off balance.

Immediately she jumps to her feet and follows up with an elbow to his left cheek and he crumples to the ground. She pulls the surgeon's lab coat up over his head then kicks him in the stomach for good measure. The pair race through the door and slam it shut behind them then Katja mashes the buttons on the security keypad until it beeps erratically.

She rubs at the side of her head. "We couldn't have just *pretended* that you attacked me?"

"I didn't . . . I mean . . ."

"You hit like a girl," she says, crossing the room towards the small staircase which is the only way out. She climbs a few steps then stops.

"What are you just standing there for?" she asks. "You coming or not?"

Nikolai shrugs. "I need the money."

"Jesus, Nikolai, you can't stay here now. Look at the pictures on his wall there—you really think that he just wants to run a few blood tests on you?"

Nikolai considers this for a few moments then follows her up the stairs.

At the top is another door with a keypad mounted on the wall beside it but this one has a green *unlock* button illuminated on it. Katja presses it and there's a heavy *thunk* then the door springs opens a half inch. The muffled sounds of the club music trickle back in. She pushes the door open the rest of the way and it leads out into a short, white corridor lined with doors. All closed.

"Come on," she says, moving up the passageway.

Each door they pass has a small blacked-out window cut into it and from within there's the sound of skin on skin, of skin on latex, and of latex on latex. They head straight for the exit but when they get there realize there's no handle on the door, just another keypad.

"Shit," Katja mutters.

"What do we do?" Nikolai asks.

"I don't know," she says, looking back down the corridor as if another exit would miraculously appear through force of their desperation.

Then there's the sound of one of the doors behind them opening, laughter spilling out from within.

"Quick, just try a combination," Nikolai says.

"Yeah, it's not like it's going to be alarmed or anything."

"Katja, they're going to find . . ."

And the door in front of them unlocks.

They both freeze, aware that there is no other escape

other than back into the surgery, Nikolai expecting to see the nurse's pink hair and purple gloved hands, but instead it's a man, pale and shifty, rubbing between thumb and forefinger one of the beaded necklaces he wears.

"Excuse me," he says, standing to one side and avoiding eye contact. Beyond him is the heavy electronic heartbeat of the club and the rainbow neon seeping into the medicinally blank corridor.

Katja and Nikolai say nothing as they push past him, leaving him to whatever corrupt deeds he was hoping to find in the corridor beyond.

15.

A fresh glass of whiskey in her hands and all thought of Stasko and the punk girl gone from her mind, Bridget looks at Liz's text message.

Caught Mr. Right. U won't believe it.

She flips her phone shut, crosses to the TVs.

She smacks one of them to stop the image sliding up and down, forcing it to settle into place.

She adjusts the contrast dial until the apartment comes into view, Liz in the background pouring some drinks. She hands a glass to a tall man and then clinks it against her own, tilting her head coquettishly.

She beckons him to follow her with a curled forefinger and leads him towards the bedroom.

Bridget switches to another screen in time to see them enter and recognises the resemblance to Johnny Cash— no wonder Liz picked him. His facial features aren't clear enough to get a good impression of them but the black shirt and bolo, black trousers, spiked cowboy boots, and quiffed hair certainly didn't do him any harm in her selection.

Liz pulls him towards her by his bolo tie then starts to unbutton his shirt but the man pushes her hands away whilst kissing her. There's just the slightest moment of worry, long enough for the feeling to make its way through the TV screen and into Bridget, but then Liz smiles. The man removes her T-shirt and says something. She lays herself down on the bed. He removes her trainers and jeans then slips off the bolo tie. He takes her hands, raises them above her head, pressing the wrists together. He leans in to kiss her and as he does so he wraps the bolo around them, knotting them together and to the bed frame.

Liz's legs, clamped together, twist from side to side, a sign, Bridget knows, of her growing lust.

The man runs a hand across her stomach and then down her legs. He clasps her crossed ankles in one hand and slips his belt from his trousers with the other then ties it around them and to the foot of the bed. Liz arches herself towards him as he hovers above her. He kisses her on the stomach, his hands lingering over her as if he were performing a psychic surgery on her. He circles around her, almost out of sight, stops by the dresser at the very edge of the screen.

He opens the drawers of the units one by one then takes something out. It looks like lipstick. He glances over his shoulder at Liz then begins to write on the mirror.

Bridget leans in to see what he is doing but he is blocking her view.

He finishes and caps the lipstick then returns it to the drawer. Steps to one side and finally Bridget can see what he has written.

SHE'S MINE NOW.

And the man is looking right at the camera.
The screen goes dead.

16.

She runs the short distance to Liz's apartment, along the street and up the stairwell which she had more often seen through the grainy CCTV footage than in person, stopping when she reaches the door, gasping for breath. She presses an ear to the door and listens for any sound coming from within.

Nothing.

She reaches up and runs a hand across the top of the door frame, finds Liz's spare key wedged into a little gap in the plaster up there. She fumbles with it in the lock, her hands shaking uncontrollably, panic welling within her. She opens the door and bursts in, calling Liz's name but getting no reply.

The only light is that coming from the bedroom.

She calls Liz's name again.

Nothing.

She realizes she has no weapon and looks around for something but all she can find is a small umbrella. She picks it up and crosses to the bedroom.

"Liz?" she asks shakily, hopefully.

She eases the bedroom door open.

Liz's clothes remain scattered across the floor but there is no sign of her or the man. Even the bolo and belt are gone. Bridget looks up at where they had hidden the camera but all that remains is a spray of fractured wires spilling from the small hole in the wall into which the device had been placed.

Then she turns to the dresser, to the message the man had scrawled there—and finds it has been added to. In smaller letters underneath the original message:

YOU CAN HAVE HER WHEN YOU BRING ME THE PUNK.

2 HOURS. ALLEY BEHIND LINDENMUTH BLVD.

The note is signed *LADY D.*

Bridget clutches a hand to her mouth. She should never have let her pick the man up without her being in the club too but by the time she had gotten back from Stasko's it was too late.

She's thinking about what she's going to do when she stands on something. She picks it up—a wig, styled with copious amounts of gel into a quiff. And next to where it had been discarded, a pair of dark trousers and a shirt, a pair of black cowboy boots.

The trail of clothes leads to Liz's wardrobe, one of the doors slightly open. Bridget looks inside to find the clothes disturbed, in particular at the end where Liz kept some of Bridget's own clothes for the rare occasion she actually stayed there.

Who the fuck are you?

17.

Lady D drives past Kissy talking with a couple of college-age boys who have obviously stumbled out of the club they have been drinking in all night. Kissy gives them the flutter-eyes and ankle-tilts until she spots Lady D's van pulling in at the end of the block.

"Sorry boys, gotta go," she says, blowing them a kiss and then walking off with the most-pronounced ass-wiggle she can manage.

"Hey babes," she says when Lady D winds down her window.

"You planning on giving those boys a little shock later tonight?"

"Nah, just playing," she says.

"Kissy, the sort of games you play would break them," Lady D tells her. She rolls a throat lozenge around in her mouth. Kissy is her final collection of the night and already Lady D's mind is on the long, hot shower which awaits her at home. "So you got some sugar for me?"

"Hella yeah."

Kissy reaches into her clutch-bag and removes a thick wad of cash. As Lady D takes it she notices the fresh swelling and bruising on Kissy's knuckles.

"They took a little convincing?"

"They took a little reminding that a debt is a debt," Kissy tells her.

Lady D drops the cash into a bag sitting on the seat beside her but not before fishing a couple of notes out and handing them back to Kissy. "Here. Get that broken nail sorted and Frenched. Granny Cilla will take care of you, just let her know I sent you."

"Thanks."

"Can't have my girls not looking the part," Lady D says, staring off into the distance.

Kissy slides the notes into her top. "You okay, Delicious? You seem a little distracted."

"I'm fine."

"Anyways, that girl we . . . uhh . . . chatted with earlier?"

"The punk?"

Kissy nods. "Yeah, look, I think I saw her—in Flesh Heel."

"Performing?"

"No," Kissy tells her, her tone more serious now. "She was brought in by this other woman and she looked drunk or something. I still recognised her though. Definitely the one we spoke to earlier."

Lady D shrugs. "If that's her way of dealing with it then that's her way. As long as she makes the gig tonight and pays up . . ."

"That's the thing," Kissy interrupts. "She *seemed* drunk—but I don't think she was. The woman that brought her in . . ."

"What about her?"

"I recognised her. She works at a little plastic surgery across town—dyed pink hair and legs to die for, you can't miss her."

"So the punk is punching above her weight."

"I don't think so." She leans in conspiratorially. "I've heard rumours, Lady D."

"What kind of rumours?"

"That this clinic, it does all the usual, Botox, lipo, laser hair removal and what have you . . ."

"God bless it all."

"Well, yeah. But what I've heard is—that's not all they do. The club, Flesh Heel, that is, you get some pretty strange types in there most nights. People who aren't content to just pull on some latex and a gas mask. People who want something . . . something more permanent."

"And what's this got to do with the punk? If you think she's wanting one of these surgeries, I couldn't care less. All I'm concerned about is her paying up. So unless she's planning on blowing the money from the gig on getting a zipper stitched into her lady garden then . . ."

"From where I was standing it didn't look like it was her decision to be there. She was spaced, Delicious, totally out of it. And if the rumours about that place are true then . . . then she might not be around for the gig tonight."

Lady D takes it all in, tonguing the throat lozenge from side to side.

"I always get my money," she says, more to herself than to Kissy. "That's what I'm here to do, right? That's why I have you and the girls."

Kissy nods.

"The woman, she just hung out in the club with her doped-up girlfriend or what?"

"I only glimpsed them. They weren't there for long—at least I didn't see them for long."

"So you think she took the punk to this surgery?"

Kissy shrugs.

"So where is this place? The surgery."

"It's across town. You know *Graphite*, the tanning salon?"

"Of course."

"Next block. A little row of stores. I think there's a Chinese fruit shop a couple of doors along from it."

"And this woman, the one who had her?"

"Her name is Solderberg or something I think—something Scandinavian anyway. She's a nurse there," Kissy says, then adds, "Had a jump of the old *Botulinum* a couple of times. Their prices are quite reasonable to be honest."

"And you think they've taken the punk back there for a little extra-curricular?"

"Could be," Kissy says.

Lady D sighs deeply. "You ever wonder if it's worthwhile us spending all this time chasing other people's money?"

Kissy shrugs. "We're doing what we're here to do."

Lady D considers this in silence.

"So what are you going to do?"

"I don't know, Kissy. If I give it all up . . . then what?"

"I, uh, I meant about the punk."

"Oh," Lady D says, forcing her mind back into focus. "I'm going to make sure we get our money, what else?"

she tells Kissy, starting the van's engine. "Because that's what I'm here to do."

Kissy nods.

"I'll go take a look at the clinic, see what I can see. You got any other pickups to make this evening?"

"That's me done," Kissy says.

"Needing a lift?"

"I'm good."

"Okay," Lady D says, revving the engine. "Oh, and Kissy?" she calls out, the other Tgirl already walking away.

"Yeah?"

"Just how reasonable are their prices?"

• • •

She finds the clinic quickly, parks the van outside a diner nearby and walks across.

All the lights are out, as she would have expected, but she takes no chances. She peers in through the front window but between the glass frosting and the blinds within she can't see a thing. She listens. Nothing.

She reaches into her clutch bag and takes out a lipstick. Uncaps it and twists and, instead of a waxy block of make-up, a thin-edged blade emerges. She pokes it into the lock and works it around, hears a click. She then re-opens her bag, this time taking out a small flashlight, a small mirror, and some heel repair glue. She shines the light into the crack between the door and the frame until she finds what she is looking for, then grips the flashlight between her teeth. She uncaps the glue and squirts it over the back of the mirror then slides the mirror into the gap where she shines the light. There's a momentary glow of red laser light and she holds it there for several moments, until the glue has set. She lets it go and the mirror stays where it is.

"And . . ."

She opens the door. Silence.

Smiles to herself.

She slips inside and closes the door behind her. Mounted on the wall to one side is the alarm system, chirruping every ten seconds or so to confirm that everything is okay, that none of the detection seals have been broken.

She removes her heels, placing them at the back of the door, then makes her way up the corridor. She listens at each door along the way then opens them one by one, the flashlight lighting her way. Two small surgeries. A cleaning closet. A small cupboard with a network hub and router mounted onto a metal rack, their lights flashing away. A private office.

And nobody there.

"Damn," she says under her breath. Then louder, "Damn."

She considers her options then walks back to the front door, enters the waiting area. Using the flashlight she locates the reception desk and opens the drawers but finds only blank sheets of stationery marked with the clinic's name and a collection of pens and paper clips. Next she opens the filing cabinet behind her, having to use her lipstick tool to crack open the lock again. She flicks through surgical records until she finds a tab marked *Employees*.

She searches through the folders within and then pulls out the one stickered *Bridget Soelberg.*

She opens the folder and there is a colour photocopy of the woman's driver's license. A smooth, narrow face and bright pink hair. The address on it is illegible, however. She keeps going, stops on a tax form of some kind.

"Found you," she says aloud, making a mental note of the address.

She puts everything back where she found it, closes the drawer and leaves the reception. She picks up her heels and is about to put them on then stops. Walks back up the corridor and into the first surgery. Using the flashlight's meagre glow to navigate she goes to the glass-fronted and wall-mounted cupboards. One more use of the lipstick tool and the door pops open. She reaches in and takes out a couple of bottles labelled *Botox* as well as a some syringes in sealed packets.

"With the worry lines you're probably giving me you owe me," she says, then gets the hell out of there.

18.

There's no alarm system in Soelberg's apartment so, after satisfying herself that there's nobody home, it's a good old-fashioned lock-picking which gets her inside.

She takes out her pencil flashlight and flicks it on.

The apartment is small, the few pieces of furniture mis-matched as if gathered at random. There's a kitchenette to one side and a pair of doors leading through into a bathroom and bedroom respectively. Both are littered with clothes and makeup. She examines the cupboards and refrigerator, mainly health foods past their expiration dates, then the books which line some shelves—old school science fiction and some pulp crime. On the counter is a box of disposable latex gloves. She checks through the stack of opened mail on the kitchen counter but there's nothing of interest there so turns her attention to the trash bin.

"Hello," she says to herself, pulling out crumpled up photographs and sticky notes. The photos are obviously hand-developed, enlargements of shots taken at a distance and all of the same man—he's exiting a club, he's ordering coffee, he's adjusting his tie in a shop window. There are blurry Polaroids too, notes stickered to them with times and dates, locations.

An address.

"Is this where you are?" She vaguely recognises the street name but it's at the very edges of the city limits, too far for her to go on a whim.

She stuffs the photos and notes back into the bin then sits before a small desk with TVs stacked on top of it. She hits the power buttons but they each display only static. She fingers the slots of the VCR decks underneath, finds a tape in one of them. She powers the deck up and hits play. Whatever it is on the tape ends as soon as it starts, returning the screen to which it is hooked up to static. She hits stop then rewinds for several seconds. Hits play again.

A couple making their way up a stairwell. They stop and start kissing then the woman leads the man up out of shot. There's a moment of static then another camera angle, this one of the inside of another apartment. The couple move through it quickly. Static again. Another shot, this one looking down on a bed. The man removes the woman's clothes.

Whilst the recording continues to play, Lady D reaches for the trash and takes out one of the photos, holds it up next to the screen. The man is definitely the one from the photos. The woman is definitely *not* Soelberg.

She opens the drawers of the desk one by one, searching around inside. She finds more videotapes, each labelled with a man's name. A notepad. Then something rigid but soft. She takes it out and holds it up to her torchlight.

"You're a little freak," she says, twisting the vibrator from side to side.

She puts it back as, on screen, the man buries his face in the woman's crotch. She flips through the notepad, past shopping lists and doodles. The final page with anything on it is titled *Dream Man*. Underneath is a list of traits, bullet-pointed.

Looks—Johnny Ca$h/dark cowboy.

Smart. Wicked smart.

Eyeliner?

She puts the pad down and rewinds the tape farther, static blitzing the sweaty, entwined bodies. She hits play again and this time the shot is of a street outside a club. It's dark and the angle isn't quite right but Lady D is certain she recognises it as *Mood Lit*, a fairly upmarket place only a couple of blocks away. The man from the photos and the mystery woman emerge together then it's back to the stairwell where she had first started watching them. This time she notices something, something she had missed the first time around—the briefest of glances from the woman, right up at the camera.

"You know," Lady D says. "*You* know . . . but he doesn't does he?"

The shot cuts to the apartment then to the bedroom. Lady D hits the pause button, freezing the man with one of the woman's ankles in each hand.

She flicks off the torchlight, sits in the darkness as she considers her next move.

She paces the length of the apartment as she thinks.

She could wait for Soelberg to return, of course, but there is no guarantee of when that would be, or even if she will return at all.

She could just forget all about Katja and see what happens, if the punk turns up for the gig to honour her debt and then deal with her if she doesn't, but the risk of Katja vanishing was too great. Lady D has a reputation to uphold.

Her pacing brings her to the apartment door and she thinks she hears something outside. She presses an ear to the door, realizes it is someone a couple of flights up, their keys jangling. She pulls away and there is something stuck to her face.

Another note.

It must have been slapped onto the back of the door. She peels it off and shines the light on it.

Tired waiting for u. Off to ML to find Dream Man. Txt u later. Liz.

Lady D crushes the note in her fist. "Time to get changed," she says.

19.

Lady D is gone, at least for now.

Lady D is now, she has decided, Jake.

He feels an urge to pull at the bolo tie and loosen it but resists, aware that the woman named Liz is now approaching him.

He subtly tugs at his crotch, hating the feeling of being loose in there and not strapped into a gaff as he had been earlier that night. His feet are aching within the boots which may well have fitted him once but haven't been worn in so long that they appear to have shrunk through disuse. The wig he wears, smeared in aged Brylcreem, itches at his scalp.

Liz is beside him now, leaning over the counter. She's dressed simply, in jeans and a tight-fitting t-shirt which shows off her tattoos. Her hair is glossy-black, her lips the deep red of viral blood. She glances briefly at him, looks away deliberately, then orders a rum and coke for herself.

"Can I get you . . . anything?" she asks suddenly.

When Jake looks up at her she's grinning sheepishly, looking as if she wished she'd never asked the question. He forces her.

"I'm sorry?"

"A drink," she says, smiling a tipsy, crooked smile. "You're . . . you're empty."

She nods at the glass in front of him, the remainder of a whiskey nothing more than a single drop of amber fluid.

"Oh," he says, feigning surprise. "Sorry. I was miles away."

"What you drawing?"

She looks down at the doodles on the napkins spread out before him. He'd made them before coming out, copying them from a book, and he'd spent the previous twenty minutes tracing over them but she doesn't need to know that. A mixture of lines and undulating curves angling away from one another, scattered with letters and symbols.

"Oh," Jake says, doing his best to look caught out. "They're called Feynman diagrams. They represent the behaviour of . . . of subatomic particles. The . . . uh . . . the blue wave represents a photon. The green squiggle is a gluon."

She raises an eyebrow but still looks interested. "And you come to a bar to draw these?"

Jakes puts on his best sheepish smile, avoiding eye contact with her, ensuring that he appears slightly shy and uncertain of himself. He'll switch it up to a more domineering stance later but for now the woman needs to feel it's her drawing him in, not the other way around.

"I guess I come to meet people," he says. "But it doesn't always work out that way."

"Too much time doodling and not enough talking?" she says.

"Probably."

The barman delivers her drink and she signals to him to wait. "So how about we do some talking?"

"Sure," Jake says. "That'd be nice."

He curls up the napkins and puts them in his pocket, taking long enough to do so that she will notice his hands. He's made a good job of the nail polish, expertly applied then chipped away at the ends to make it look as if he has been wearing it for several days. The barman slides another whiskey in front of him.

So they start talking just like she suggested, Jake sticking with the slightly awkward demeanour he'd decided on, letting her lead the conversation as she gradually gets closer and closer to him.

"Can I get you another drink?" he asks her eventually. Four empty glasses are lined up before her.

"Sure," she says and he notices her pupils are now fully dilated.

"But not here."

"Then where?" Liz dips a finger into the bottom of her glass then slips the tip of it into her mouth, a little girl gesture and maybe she is performing as much as he is.

"Do you have somewhere we can go?"

"Yeah," she says, then the coquettishness falls away. "Look, I don't normally do this . . ."

"But sometimes things just click into place," Jake finishes for her. "The superposition collapses."

He smiles at his own absurdity and she bursts out laughing, leaning her head into him, her hand on his back.

"Exactly," she says, looking him right in the eyes. "I was just going to say that myself."

She laughs again and then kisses him.

When she pulls away her expression is more serious, assessing his reaction to what she has just done.

Jake reaches out and takes her hand.

"Then lets get out of here," he says.

20.

Bridget kills the car's engine but remains seated within it, her breath coming fast and sharp, almost painfully so. Her heart thuds in her chest and she can almost feel the blood rushing through the veins and arteries in her neck and temples. Her hands are shaking.

She still doesn't know exactly how she is going to do this, to get Katja back from Stasko. Could she really expect to just walk back in there and ask for her back? Or threaten Stasko? Or somehow smuggle her out? Either would mean the end of everything as it stands.

But all she can think about is Liz.

Her eyes are red and raw from wiping away panicked tears on the drive across. Her mouth is dry.

She gets out of the car and walks to Flesh Heel, avoiding eye contact with the doormen on duty though they will obviously recognise her. Inside the place is still busy though the headache-inducing Euro-synth has now been replaced by retro goth and new romantic tracks. She heads straight for the door at the rear. Her hands linger over the keypad.

She considers, for the first time, what Stasko's plans for the punk might be and how far into his planned surgeries he will be. Will she even be recognisable as the girl which Bridget had earlier delivered?

She punches in the secure code and slowly descends the stairs.

She doesn't call out his name, not yet, perhaps hoping that the punk will be there by herself, briefly worrying that the punk might not be there at all.

The gurney is empty but the sheets atop it are ruffled. The machines around it look as if they have been hurriedly shoved out of the way. Bridget descends the rest of the way, still remaining as quiet as she can.

"Doctor?"

She notices something smeared across the ground next to the observation room and approaches slowly. It looks like toothpaste which has been spat out and left to dry.

"Doctor?" she asks again but still no reply. Maybe he's gone back to the clinic to get additional equipment or off to one of his dealers for black market drugs. Perhaps she will be able to just sneak the girl back out after all.

She presses her face to the observation room's window and peers in.

And sees Stasko sprawled on the ground.

She punches in the security code and throws open the door. A long smear of blood on the waxy floor beneath him indicates that he has dragged himself, or been dragged, towards the door.

"Doctor!" she calls out and rushes to his side.

He blinks to clear his vision, his thoughts. He holds out one hand and Bridget takes it.

"Bridget?"

"What happened?"

"The girl," he says as she helps him to his feet. He touches his ear, clotted with dried blood, winces. "That fucking man."

"What man?" she asks, wondering if he meant the man from the club, if he'd tracked down Katja before she could. But she came straight to Flesh Heel from the apartment, he couldn't possibly have gotten there before her.

"The one you brought!" he shouted at her, pushing her away.. He sways, still woozy and now without her for support. He leans on the counter behind him, smearing blood on it.

"Where is she?" Bridget asks. "What did she do to you?"

"She's gone!" he screams and Bridget feels something plummet deep within her chest.

"She's gone?" Bridget says, trying to get her head around the concept and what it means. "She . . . she can't be gone . . ."

"Take a look around!" He switches on the tap and dabs water over his wound.

"But I have to find her."

"You're damn right you do, Nurse Soelberg," he says, switching back to the more formal method of addressing her. "That fucking junkie you brought here helped her escape. This is *your* doing, *your* responsibility. Get out of here and go find her. Bring her back to me."

Bridget's mind spins, having trouble keeping up with the night's events, now spiralling around her.

"But . . . I . . . I don't . . ."

Her words falter. She has no idea what to do now. She thinks of Liz and her panic increases.

"How am I supposed to know where—"

"*Your* problem, Nurse Soelberg," Stasko snaps, applying a cotton swab to his wound.

It was sheer luck that had enabled her to find the girl in the first place, what chance is there of her being able to do the same thing again? Particularly now that she is on the run, Katja will be even harder to find than she had been earlier. The only connection Bridget has is the squat and there is surely no way that the punk will be stupid enough to go back there, not after being grabbed from outside it—twice within ten minutes. She'll need to head for somewhere else, somewhere she can lie low and get to quickly.

Someone Nikolai can go to as well.

21.

Heading towards Lindenmuth, trailing Bridget's car at safe enough distance, Stasko still isn't sure whether he can trust her any more.

There is something about her reaction to him telling her about Katja escaping that feels wrong to him and this feeling is compounded by the fact that it was Bridget who selected the guinea pig in the first place—the guinea pig who ended up helping the punk to break free. Bridget had made it clear throughout her time with him that she didn't want any involvement in his special procedures but despite this he had always felt that he could trust her.

Now?

He sees a Policie car up ahead coming in the opposite direction and slouches a little farther into his seat until it passes.

He turns a corner, rain water spraying up side of the car as it passes through a puddle. The rain is falling again so he hits the wipers, slowing to keep a safe distance between Bridget and himself.

Up ahead, a figure emerges from between two buildings. It staggers into the illumination cast by the streetlights.

Stasko slows the car even further. Rain batters the windscreen. He squints, trying to figure out if it is just another drunk or junkie—or something more.

The figure is slim with a shaven head and wears a pair of black leggings and a tight t-shirt with a skull painted on it, now stained with blood, something wrapped around their neck.

"Katja," he says aloud.

So Bridget had been across this side of town for a good reason. She must have known, or suspected, that the punk was in the area. But how?

He stops the car and continues to watch from a distance.

The punk stumbles along the street, using the brick wall of the adjacent building to support herself, clasping a hand to her head.

Stasko flicks the headlights off, puts the car back into gear and drifts towards her.

She appears to be completely unaware of his approach despite the headlights now falling on her.

He picks up some speed but keeps it in first, the engine whining, and when he's only a few metres away she finally looks up, her eyes going wide and the car slams into her.

22.

Nikolai's squat is an old college dorm, severed from the rest of the neighbourhood in which it is nestled by an overpass that sweeps up and overhead like the light-flash of a blade. The road's support structure straddles the building on either side, fencing it in. There's a constant drip-drip of oily water from high above.

He leads Katja inside and along a wide corridor with a black and white tiled floor, the lacquer long since scrubbed away, ornate doors spaced at regular intervals. There are notice boards mounted on the walls in the gaps between the doors, a legacy from the building's previous usage, now littered with notes from the various inhabitants to and from one another—insults, love letters, threats. There are graffiti and drawings sketched onto the wall in Biro, the paint beneath chipped away. And gig posters, just like the one Nikolai had discovered earlier and torn down.

The rest of the inhabitants linger in the background and through the gaps in the doorways, as if each senses the presence of someone new and wishes to keep their distance. They pass one room marked with double doors, and Katja glances through the little windows nestled into it. It's blindingly bright inside, the outline of huge lamps only just visible, and she recognises the stench of homegrown instantly. A girl in her late teens, all plump lips and rock-steady attitude, strides past in bright pink canvas boots. She's chewing gum and pops the bubble she has been working on as she passes them.

They keep walking.

Nikolai leads her down a short set of steps and into what was once an office. The furniture has been shoved to one side, snapped and broken where necessary, replaced with a couple of sofa beds, a small lamp, a CD player and a stack of CDs. A small chest of drawers and a couple of shelves. Katja notices a set of drumsticks in a plastic jug. Nikolai sees her looking at them but doesn't say anything.

"You okay?" he asks instead.

"Yeah," she says, shrugging. She surveys the room, picking up CDs and plucking books from a shelf just to have something to do.

"Your neck . . ."

She touches a finger to her throat and it comes away tacky. She pulls at the dressing and drops it into a bin full of empty energy drink cans.

"You sure it's safe here?" she asks him.

"Yeah," he says without particular conviction. He closes the door as if to reassure her.

"I just got sick of hiding, Nik," Katja says, unprompted. She looks into a mirror, blurry with fingerprints. She tilts her head from side to side, running a hand across her shaven scalp and neck tattoo. "I guess I knew the posters would be a risk even after doing this to myself—but what the fuck else am I good for?"

She touches the new trach tube emerging from her throat and she reluctantly admits to herself that it does actually look quite good.

"Why do you think he took you? The surgeon."

"Who knows," she says. "There was some other guy in a raincoat too."

"So what now?"

"Now I lay low until the gig."

"You can't still go ahead with it—who knows who else has recognised you?"

"I told you already, I've had enough of hiding, Nikolai. I need the money but more than that I need to play again. It's the only time I feel worth a shit."

"And it's worth the risk?"

"You either take control or others do," she says.

She opens the drawers of the chest unit one by one, plucking items of clothing from it then pulls off her skull t-shirt, unties her boots and wriggles out of her leggings. Nikolai finds sudden interest in the posters on the walls as she stands before him in her underwear.

"The fat guy, the one who jumped me in the first place, he knew who I was or at least he said he did. He knew about the island."

"A friend of Szerynski or one of the other dealers?"

"Who knows. He stank of cop," she says. She selects a pair of baggy cargo pants and pulls them on. They slouch on her hips even after she pulls the belt tight.

Next is a similarly oversized hooded top, black with a design which has flaked away. When she puts it on all shape is lost from her body. She laces her boots back up and lets the cargos drop down over them, almost entirely concealing them.

"Whoever he was, if he knows about my involvement in what went on then he probably knows about yours too."

"What about the surgeon? He didn't recognise me. And he didn't seem to know who you were either."

She nods, accepting this. "Who knows what that freak wanted or why? Point is it could have just been luck that Fatso found me. Someone could have tipped him off about the squat and he knew that if he waited long enough I'd turn up. If he knew about the gig then he probably would have just waited and come for me there instead."

"That still doesn't mean it's safe to go through with it."

"You got a razor?"

He points to a plastic cup. Inside is a worn toothbrush, a nail file, and disposable razor. She takes the razor and goes back to the mirror, starts shaving her scalp.

"Anyway, the tranny has my guitar and if I don't do the gig then I can't get it back. And while we're there you can tell her that the debt is yours."

"We?"

"You're coming too", she says, tapping the razor to get rid of crumbly shavings.

"I am?"

"It's your debt that's gotten me into this mess in the first place isn't it? You come down there and tell that psycho cross-dresser that this all has nothing to do with me. Don't worry, once it's all sorted we'll go our separate ways and I'll be out of your life again."

"Oh."

"What?"

"Nothing," he says. "I was just going to say . . . I could probably sort you out with a space here. If you needed it. Or wanted it."

She looks at the two beds.

"Oh, I didn't mean . . . I just meant in the building."

She shakes her head. "I'll figure something out myself. All that matters just now is getting through the next few hours. They might have figured out where I'm staying but at least they won't know where you are."

"Right," he says. "You mean the fat guy."

"And the surgeon."

"And the surgeon," he repeats. Then something obviously occurs to him. "Well . . ."

Katja puts the razor down. Turns. "They couldn't possibly know where you stay, right? We made sure nobody followed us."

Nikolai wriggles. Katja fixes him with a stare, takes a pace towards him. He takes a pace back.

"Nik."

"The form," he says. "The release form. The nurse that picked me up made me fill it out and it asked for my . . ."

"*You gave them your fucking address? This address?*"

"Well, the form asked for it."

"Jesus *fucking* Christ," Katja says, already making her way out of the room.

Nikolai chases after her. "I'm sure it'll be fine, they probably won't even . . ."

"Won't even what?" she says, turning abruptly. "They won't bother to come *looking*? Nikolai, you're as big a fuck-up as ever, you know that? We've got to get out of here *now*."

She climbs the short set of steps leading into the main corridor, leaving him behind.

Then stops suddenly.

A few metres in front of her, looking as shocked as Katja herself, is a woman in her early thirties.

Pink hair and purple latex gloves.

23.

Spending so much time in amongst the guinea pig community, Bridget has figured out how to let herself blend in with them and so despite still being dressed in her work uniform and heels she manages to enter the squat without raising suspicion. It's all about the attitude.

Once inside it's a trickier prospect, no real idea of where to go and not wanting to start asking at random in case any alarms are triggered, so she walks up the main corridor as if she knows exactly where she is going. One hand clutching her jacket pocket, feeling the outline of the syringe she has brought with her. Her heels clatter off the floor, accompanying the incessant *tap-tap* of the water drops falling onto the building's roof. She's holding her panic in check, trying not to think about where Liz might be or what whoever took her might be doing with her.

Her only thoughts are of the punk.

And here she is, emerging from a staircase up ahead.

Despite wearing what appears to be the clothing of a sixteen-stone man the recognition is instantaneous, the image of her from the poster now burned into Bridget's mind. Katja was unconscious when Bridget stole her from the fat man and only minimally conscious as she led her through Flesh Heel but this doesn't matter. The punk knows.

Standing there, facing each other. Frozen.

Bridget's only way of getting Liz back safely.

Katja turns and runs up the corridor, Bridget already giving chase, pulling the syringe from her pocket. The baggy trousers appear to impede the punk's progress, constantly snagging beneath her boots and threatening to trip her up and so despite her heels Bridget soon catches up with her, launching herself when within reach. The two come crashing to the ground. Bridget tugs the plastic cap from the tip of the syringe and spits it out, then raises it ready to plunge into the soft flesh at the back of Katja's neck but at the last moment she spots someone standing behind her.

Then something smashes into the side of her head and throws her sideways.

A loud and intense ringing echoes through one ear and for several seconds she can't focus. She clasps the side of her head but there's no blood. The syringe lies a few feet away, intact. Through the ringing she hears footsteps and looks up in time to see Katja running off in the opposite direction, back towards the front door, accompanied by a skinny man who glances over his shoulder, only briefly, but still long enough for her to recognise him as the guinea pig.

Nikolai. The one who had led her to Katja in the first place. Who has led her to Katja for a second time.

Bridget tries to get up but her head feels as if it has become enveloped in a thick mist. Unconsciousness threatens. She slides to the floor and remains there. When she finally gets up again there's no sign of the two, only a big guy with long blonde hair and a scraggy blonde beard looking down at her with vague interest, sucking the remains of a huge cup of cola through a straw. The drink rasps as it empties. He shakes it to check there is nothing left then puts it on a ledge and wanders off, his interest in her lost.

Bridget gets to her feet, having to lean on the wall for support. She retrieves the syringe then looks down the empty corridor.

There's no time to go chasing after them.

Her only chance may now be gone. The punk is gone. And Liz?

The two had emerged from a staircase to one side so she heads towards it, sliding herself along the wall and down the steps until her balance recovers. There are only a couple of doors in the short passageway which the steps lead to and only one of those is open. She presses two fingers to it, pushing it open while still keeping her distance from whatever may lie within, the syringe raised in one gloved hand.

A few seconds pass, no sounds, no movement and nobody jumping out at her.

She opens the door the rest of the way and goes inside.

The room is small and cluttered, two sofa beds on either side of her and miscellanea scattered around them. And next to a chest of drawers, some clothing. The clothing the punk had been wearing earlier that night—

black leggings and a skull t-shirt. Bridget picks them up and lays them on one of the beds. She looks around to find some clue as to where the two might have gone but knowing that she has probably already been granted all the lucky coincidences she is due, at least for the time being.

There's nothing of use to her.

The panic is rising again and she checks her watch to see how long she has left.

Why does everyone want the punk so badly?

She hears a noise outside and backs up behind the door. Someone coming down the steps, walking past the room. She peers through the tiny gap between the door and the hinges.

It can't be.

Katja . . . has come back?

Bridget remains still, even holding her breath, not wanting to make a single sound.

Has she assumed that Bridget will have chased after them and so doubled-back, thinking that the safest place to hide again might be the most obvious place? Or is she just so cocky as to not realize the stupidity of taking such a risk?

Bridget edges her way around the door, half-expecting Katja to jump out at her but nothing happens. One of the other doors, previously closed, is now open an inch. Bridget slips off her heels and walks towards it, the syringe still primed in one hand, her footfalls now silent. She can hear someone inside, a clicking noise.

She shoves open the door and charges inside, spotting someone at the corner of the room, a stack of CDs in their hands. They look up at her, the CD's falling from their hands and crashing to the floor.

"What the fu . . . ?"

Not Katja. Not even female. The same height and build, yes. But not her.

For a time the two don't move, Bridget standing there with the syringe in hand and the squatter still mentally processing exactly what the fuck is going on.

"I was only going to borrow them. . . ." he says, holding his hands up in submission.

Of course she wouldn't come back, at least not so soon. Of course she wouldn't.

And now what? Bridget thinks.

The man's hair is short and wiry, sticking out at odd angles, and yet the impression of him looking like Katja isn't going away. His features are small and defined, quite feminine.

"Look, I'm just going to split, okay. . . ."

And he's coming towards her, hands still held up in submission. Bridget lets him. Her hand tightens on the syringe.

He moves past her, avoiding any eye contact, probably used to the array of freaks and psychos who inhabited places such as this, just wanting to keep his head down and get out of there.

Bridget grabs him, pulls him in towards her. He cries out but she muffles it with one hand whilst the other plunges the needle into his neck and even as she does it she's still not entirely sure why. He's too shocked to struggle at first and by the time realisation sets in the drug is already coursing through his system, shutting it down piece by piece like streetlights during a blackout.

He slumps in her arms and Bridget has to catch him, the needle still sticking out of his neck. She slips her hands under him and drags him out and into what she assumes is Nikolai's room, lets him flop onto one of the beds. She closes the door. Her breath comes sharp and fast as she looks down at him. She runs a hand across her face, wiping away sweat from her upper lip.

Then she takes off his clothes, the ratty trousers and dark grey top, stretched and split around the collar. She dresses him in Katja's clothes, having to fight a little to get the leggings over his slightly broader thighs. She plucks the syringe from his neck and his head flops to one side. Traces a hand across his hair.

She looks around and spots the razor on top of the dresser, grabs it, then starts shaving the man's head. The razor is near-blunt and tugs at his scalp and for a while he looks like an alopecia sufferer but with a little effort and a bit of lubrication in the form of spit she manages to finish it off. Far from perfect but it's the best she can do.

She takes a step back, tilting her head to one side. Squinting.

Yes, he looks vaguely like Katja, and yes, he has the same slender, angular build—but he's clearly not her.

"Shit," Bridget says aloud. Checks her watch again.

She holds her hands up, normally as steady as Stasko's but now quivering and jumping.

And then it occurs to her.

Each day she assists the surgeon in adjusting people or transforming them completely. The answer is obvious.

She looks around then spots an ornament, tipped over next to the bed. It's a small sculpture of what is possibly a bear but there are fragments missing, broken off, leaving rough edges behind. She picks it up and it's heavy.

Looks back at the squatter, laying on the bed as if merely passed out from a night of excess.

"I'm sorry," Bridget says then smashes the ornament into his face.

24.

A patrol car lines up alongside her as she waits at a junction and Bridget leans forward to block the officer's view of the drugged and beaten body in the passenger seat should he look across at her.

She stares at the traffic lights suspended above the wet street, pointedly not making eye contact with the officer, willing the lights to change. Then she can't help it and briefly glances to the side.

The officer is laughing and there's the sound of radio chatter. His eyes nail hers.

He frowns, then smiles.

Bridget forces a smile back.

The lights change but neither of them move and she's thinking, *Is this a test? What does he want me to do?*

Act normal. Act normal.

She eases onto the gas, lets the clutch drop and leaves the patrol car behind, all the while her attention going to the road ahead then to her side mirror and back again. A moment later and the cop is moving too. She waits for its lights to start flashing, grinding her teeth in anticipation, before he peels off into a side street and is gone.

Despite her desire to floor it she keeps her speed steady and well under the limit, not wanting to draw any attention to herself, all the way to Lindenmuth Blvd. She pulls up next to a scrapyard encircled by patchwork fencing and stolen street signs then switches the engine off. Parked halfway up an alley at the side of the yard is a white van with huge red lips spray-painted across the rear doors.

Bridget gets out then circles around and opens the passenger door.

The guy is still out of it and she hopes it is just from the injection than the beating which followed. She touches two fingers to his neck and finds a weak pulse.

She'd done the best she could to distort his features without doing any serious damage. Both cheeks are swollen and one is split. A large bruise darkens the left side of his face, accompanied by a rather prominent lump which looks like a marble has been inserted under his skin. There's dried blood on his nose and forehead. She's also wrapped a scarf she'd had in the back of her car around the man's neck to cover the plain flesh where there should have been a tattoo and a trach tube.

This is never going to work.

But then what other choice does she have?

She hooks an arm under the man and lifts him out, glad for his slight build. Drags him up the alley.

As she approaches, someone gets out of the van—a tall, broad woman wearing a tight black cocktail dress with a purple sash and a pair of elbow-length satin gloves. The woman looks as if she has just stepped out of a ballroom.

Bridget hesitates, wondering if she has gotten the wrong location.

The woman drops a cigarette to the ground and crushes it under one foot. Motions for Bridget to come towards her.

Bridget struggles the rest of the way up the alley and its only as she gets closer that she realizes the woman is not, at least in the strictest sense, a woman. And she thinks of the discarded clothing and wig, the raided wardrobe. Liz's dress?

She lets the squatter slump to the ground beside her. "Lady D?"

The transvestite tilts her head to one side, the way a dog might when hearing a familiar word, looking at what Bridget has brought her.

"Sorry for the mess," Bridget says. "But she wasn't for coming voluntarily."

Lady D continues to examine the body from a distance. Takes a step closer. Bridget holds up a hand.

"Where's Liz?"

"In the van."

"Is she okay?"

Lady D nods at the body. "I was just about to ask you the same thing."

"She's fine. Out cold but nothing serious."

"You better be sure about that."

"I want to see her. Liz. Now."

"She doesn't even look alive."

For a split second Bridget panics then realizes the Tgirl is referring to the body, not Liz.

"She's alive."

"Forgive me if I'm not going to take your word for it."

Lady D takes a step forward. Bridget matches her, blocking her view of the body now.

"I want to see her first," she says.

Lady D mulls it over then nods. She opens the rear door of the van just a little, pokes her head in and mutters a warning, then opens it the rest of the way. Liz emerges from the darkness. Her hands are bound and makeup smears her face. There are streaks of red around her mouth that could be lipstick or could be blood.

A wave of anger, sadness and fear hits Bridget and she only just manages to swallow it down before the van door is slammed shut again.

"If you've hurt her . . ."

"I hardly think you're one to talk, Nurse Soelberg."

The use of her name sends a shiver up Bridget's spine but she says nothing as the transvestite approaches, bends down next to the body. She turns its head from side to side, examining the wounds and, thankfully, chooses the wrist to measure for a pulse instead of removing the scarf. Bridget looks at the van, resisting the urge to run to the vehicle and grab Liz before Lady D realizes Liz's deceit.

"She's alive. That's good enough for me."

Lady D picks the body up, hooking one arm around her shoulder just as Bridget had but carrying it with far more ease. She opens the van door and puts the body inside, then motions for Liz to come and helps her out of the van. Liz stands there for a moment, not sure what to do.

"Off you go," Lady D says, easing her forward.

Bridget locks on to Liz's eyes, encouraging her to keep

coming as if her gaze is a homing beacon. As soon as she is close enough, Bridget grabs and embraces her.

"We're done?" Bridget asks.

Lady D closes the door, her chest and silk gloves now smeared with blood. "Done," she confirms. "Nice doing business with you."

And she just stands there, arms crossed, until Bridget and Liz turn and walk back up the alley.

They keep walking at a steady pace, around the corner to Bridget's Honda. Bridget fumbles for her keys then opens the passenger door and helps Liz inside, circles around and climbs into the driver's seat. Once they are inside she finally feels able to speak.

"Are you okay? Did he hurt you?"

Liz shakes her head even as Bridget checks her over, gently touching the other woman's face and glad to find that the discolouration is all just make-up.

"I'm okay," Liz says. "Just a little shaken. Do you have anything to . . . ?"

She holds up her wrists, still bound with cable ties. Bridget leans across and retrieves a small knife from the glove box, slices through the plastic. Liz rubs at her reddened, raw skin.

"What the fuck was that all about?"

"I don't know," Bridget says, looking through the rear window to see if there is any sign of the van.

"You don't *know*? It's something to do with Stasko isn't it?"

"I think so," Bridget says but leaves it at that.

"Fuckin' asshole." Liz twists the rear-view mirror to face her and examines herself.

"Who was that you . . . gave her? Him. *Her*."

"Nobody important."

"They seemed important to him. To *her*."

"That's the problem."

"What problem?"

"It's not who she thinks it is. It's not who she wanted."

Liz twists the rear view back. She checks over her shoulder too. "What do you mean, not who she wanted? And what do you keep looking at?"

"I had to do it," Bridget explains. "To get you back, I mean. She wanted this girl and—look, it's complicated but bottom line is it's only a matter of time until she realizes that I've fucked her over. I couldn't bring her the girl so I improvised. Not to mention Stasko . . ."

Her phone rings. She pulls it out of her pocket.

Stasko.

"Bridget?"

Ringing.

"What's going on?"

"I have to . . ."

And Bridget hits the button to pick up the call.

"Where are you? Have you found her?" he barks down the line.

"Not yet," Bridget says, side-stepping his initial question.

"What about the address? You said that . . ."

"They're not there. They must have known we'd come looking for them."

There are a few moments of silence, enough for Bridget to wonder if he knows exactly what is going on.

"Where are you?"

And this time she can't avoid it.

"Back of Lindenmuth."

"What the hell are you doing over there?"

"Looking," she says simply. Checks the rear window again. Liz stares at her with an expression she can't quite read.

"I'll be there in ten minutes."

"What for? If we're going to find her then . . ."

"I'm already on my way, Bridget."

Then he hangs up.

"What the fuck is going on?" Liz demands as soon as Bridget puts the phone down.

"We have to get out of here."

"Is she coming?" Liz asks, craning to see out the window.

"I mean the city, we have to get out of the city," Bridget says. "Together."

Liz is about to say something but stops. Her frown softens, disappears. Bridget looks right at her.

"It was never the men I was watching," Bridget says. Then she peels off one of her gloves and looks at her hand as if it isn't really a part of her. She reaches across and touches Liz's cheek.

"Where would we go?" Liz asks after a few seconds, reluctant to risk her talking breaking the contact and grateful when it remains.

"We'll figure something out. Do you have somewhere safe you could go for a couple of days?"

"I don't know . . . maybe."

"I've got money but it's going to take me a day or so to sort things out."

"I could probably crash with—"

"Don't tell me," Bridget interrupts. "It's better if I don't know. Stasko's on his way here—wherever it is can you go there now? And just lay low until you hear from me."

"Bridget what have you gotten yourself involved with?"

"I have no idea," Bridget says. "Just say you'll come with me?"

Liz puts a hand over Bridget's, still cupping her face. Then she leans across and kisses Bridget.

"I'll come with you."

25.

DeBoer is standing in a queue at an all-night pharmacy, resisting scratching his asshole, when his phone chimes.

He checks the number before answering. Unidentified.

He picks up but doesn't say anything.

"Umm . . . Detective DeBoer?" the voice on the other end of the line says.

Male. Not young, not old, but anywhere in between. DeBoer doesn't recognise it.

"And you are?" DeBoer asks, finally giving in and clawing at his backside. Relief floods through him and a strange, blissful twitching affects one eye. He hums with joy until he catches the scruffy teen in front of him looking over his shoulder.

"The fuck you looking at?" he snaps at the man.

And, just as expected, the relief is short-lived, quickly chased down and enveloped by an angry, burning pain that shoots up his asshole, spreading into his gut. He clenches his buttcheeks and teeth simultaneously.

"I'm sorry?" the caller says.

"Not you. So who is this?"

"A friend of a friend," the caller says.

The line moves forward by one person, agonisingly slowly. The fiery pain is fading now, the background itching drone returning.

"I have lots of friends," DeBoer says.

"Yeah, well. I'd heard you were looking for someone."

DeBoer remains silent, staring at the back of the head of the old woman explaining what she is needing to the pharmacist and not being particularly successful.

"A, uh, a woman?"

"Look, buddy, I'm kind of busy right now. Cut to the cheese, pal."

"I know where she is. I know who has her."

DeBoer's attention is finally gotten but he still says nothing. Waits.

"There's a debt collector. A transvestite called Lady—"

"Delicious," DeBoer says, moving forwards now that the old lady is gone. Only two more in front of him.

"You know her?"

"I told you already I have lots of friends," the detective replies. "So what makes you think she has the punk?"

"Because I just saw her being handed over and put in the back of Lady Delicious' van. White with a mouth painted onto the rear doors."

The scruffy teen is now being served, saying something about pus oozing from somewhere he'd rather it wasn't.

"Handed over? By who?"

"Just some woman. I don't know. Pink hair. Weird uniform."

"And this just happened? Where?"

"Over by Lindenmuth Blvd. Near the scrapyard. That's why I called you. If you hurry then—"

"And who did you say you were again?"

A pause. "A friend. Of a friend."

The teen shuffles off, avoiding eye contact with DeBoer, clutching a paper bag of creams. DeBoer steps up to the counter.

"Yes?" the pharmacist asks.

DeBoer holds up a finger to ask him to wait.

"Which friend?"

"I just heard the word is all," the caller says. "On the street, you know? Look, if you want her then you have to come now otherwise . . ."

The pharmacist. "Sir, please, how can I help you? As you can see we're very busy and tonight—"

DeBoer stabs the finger at him, turns the phone onto his shoulder. "It feels like someone has set fire to some razor wire and shoved it up my ass, okay? Is that enough fucking information for you?! And don't give me any of that over-the-counter shit either!"

"Uhmmm . . . I'm sorry I don't know what . . ." the voice on the other end of the phone is saying as he puts it back to his ears.

"Not you!" DeBoer shouts at him.

"Are you on any other medications, sir?" the pharmacist asks.

"Buddy, I can be there quickly, I'm only a couple of blocks away. But that little bitch has been giving me the runaround all night and yours is not the first tip-off I've had."

"So?"

The pharmacist. "Sir?"

"Just give me some fucking *cream*!" DeBoer shouts at him. Back to the phone. "*So, if your information isn't as good as you seem to think it is then, well . . . I won't be happy. I'll come looking for you. And when I look for something I don't stop until I fucking find it, you understand me?*"

Silence on the other end of the line. Then, faintly, "Yes."

"Good," DeBoer says.

The pharmacist. "I'm sorry sir but we have to verify that you're not going to have a reaction to anything we might give you. Can you fill out this form first so that we can—"

DeBoer's rage boils over and he punches the Plexiglass in front of him. "Fuck off then!" he shouts and punches the screen again before turning and stalking off, on his way to Lindenmuth.

26.

The station wagon's engine rattles and grinds as it comes to a halt then lets out a little burp of steam.

As DeBoer had approached Lindenmuth he'd spotted a red Honda parked up and there was enough of a glow from the nearby street lights to detail the outline of two people inside. He'd slowed slightly as he came up to the car, trying to get a look at the occupants out of the corner of his eye, then continued on for another block before circling back to the junkyard from the other side.

Now he sits in the car, thinking.

Itching. Burning.

He looks around for any other suspicious vehicles or figures but the street is dead. The one in the Honda had, at least in the brief glimpse he had gotten of them, looked like a women but there is the distinct likelihood that it could be one of Lady's D notorious transvestite crew instead. He takes the pistol from his shoulder holster and checks it. Slips it back in and starts to button his coat over it then thinks better of it. Then carefully reaches into a pocket and takes out the syringe which had earlier been stuck in him, still with a thumb's height of fluid inside the plastic chamber. Puts it back.

He gets out and casually walks towards the alley then straight past it, again relying on peripheral vision, but it's enough to let him know that the white van is still parked there, facing him. He slows after a few paces then turns back, fumbling in his pockets as if having forgotten something. Stops when he reaches the alley and peers into it.

At first all he can see is the van, then a figure emerges from behind it. Tall and broad, high-heeled and with shoulder-length blonde hair.

Lady Delicious, rummaging around in her handbag. She turns away from him and he rushes to the other side of the alley, then along the wall towards the van. He ducks underneath the driver's side window and shuffles towards the rear wheel so that his legs and feet will remain hidden. Listens.

He hears her mumbling something to herself then there's a thud against the van, coming from the inside. DeBoer jumps back in shock but doesn't move. A voice, coming from inside, too muffled to be able to tell what is being shouted. More pounding.

Then Lady Delicious's heeled footsteps, going towards the front of the van. DeBoer edges himself in the opposite direction, ending up at the rear of the vehicle. He peers around it and sees the Tgirl leaning in through the now-open passenger door, then stands on his tip-toes to see through the van's rear windows. There's movement inside, a figure lying on the ground, barely visible, but skinny and with a shaven head.

He reaches for his gun then thinks better of it. Instead he retrieves the syringe.

It is all so exquisitely perfect: to not only get his hands on the punk again but to steal her from the very one who was about to be sent to collect the debt from him—and to use the weapon which had been used to take her from him in the first place.

Footsteps again, so he retreats back around the side of the van. Crouches down, watching Lady D's incongruously muscular legs, then realizes he can see her reflected in a pane of glass which is laid up against a dumpster straight ahead. She's got a phone in her hand now and is thumbing a message or number into it. She turns away from him and he doesn't waste the opportunity, jumping around and stabbing the syringe into her neck, squeezing the end to deliver what remains of the sedative into her bloodstream. She grabs at her shoulder, tries to twist around but DeBoer has a hold of her. She claws at him blindly, one of his sleeves rucking up and her fingernails raking along his skin to ignite a line of pain but he holds firm until she slumps in his arms. The phone drops from her hand and he lets her crash to the ground, ending up folded in half, her forehead and left shoulder in contact with the ground, hair cloaking her and her ass high in the air.

DeBoer takes out his gun, edges up to the door. He listens but it's all gone quiet inside. Stands on his tip-toes again but can no longer see the figure inside. He stands as far back as he can whilst still reaching the handle then opens the door, gun pointed at the opening.

Nothing.

No one.

"Alright," he says, stepping from side to side, trying to see into the darkness. "Come on out you little bitch."

Movement, then a hand, held up high, fingers spread, quickly followed by another in a gesture of surrender.

DeBoer suddenly lunges at the punk and grabs her, pulling one arm up behind her back farther than is necessary to restrain her, smiling as she squeals in pain. He forces her towards the car, slamming her into it then throwing her into the back while she is still stunned. With his grip on her finally gone she spins around to face him.

DeBoer lowers the gun just a little. "What the fuck? Who the hell are you?"

A shaved head, yes. Skinny, yes. Wearing the same leggings and skull t-shirt as the punk. But not Katja. Not even female.

"Please . . ." the boy says, holding out his hands, shuffling closer. His face is swollen and bloody, his lips crusted with dried blood.

"Hey, hey!" DeBoer warns him, jabbing the pistol at him. "You just stay right the fuck where you are! I'm a detective, you understand?"

"I don't know what's going on," the man says, a globule of saliva dripping from his mouth. Still shuffling. "I was just . . . I mean . . . I don't even . . ."

And then before the detective knows what is happening the boy lashes out, kicking the gun from DeBoer's hand and sending it skittering across the wet pavement. DeBoer turns and the boy leaps out, knocking

DeBoer to one side before fleeing past him. The boy runs back up the alley, leaps over Lady Delicious' still-prone form, collides with the wall and the van then is gone. DeBoer recovers his weapon and gives chase but he gets wedged in the small gap between alley and van. He tries to squeeze through, his raincoat snagging, eventually having to take it off to free himself but by then the boy is long gone.

"Motherfucker," DeBoer growls.

He still isn't sure what's going on, whether the informant has set him up or not, but what he does know is when it is time to get the hell out of somewhere. He goes back around the other side of the van, stops by the driver's door. Opens it. When he leans in his main intent is to hope the vehicle's keys are there and either steal them or just take the van but those plans vanish at the sight of the bags lying in the footwell. Three of them. He reaches in and pulls one of them across.

It's stuffed with money.

He grabs all of them, calculating how much might be inside. Twenty thousand at least—maybe thirty? Enough to cover his debts plus a little extra, and though maybe not as much as the punk might have brought him it's certainly far less trouble.

He snatches the bags then hurries back to the station wagon, deciding that Lady Delicious can keep her fucking van. He has what he needs—now all he has to do is clear what he owes before anyone realizes how he has been able to do so.

27.

Stasko flicks the headlights back on then rushes around to where the punk's body lies, hoping that he's hit her hard enough to floor her without doing any major damage.

She groans, holding her leg. Rolls onto her back.

"What the fuck is going *on* tonight?" she says.

No. *He* says.

The boy holds one hand up against the glare of the headlights to protect swollen and bruised eyes, injuries that look as if they were there prior to the impact of Stasko's car.

"You're wearing her . . . her clothes," Stasko says as the realisation hits.

The man sits up before suddenly crying out in pain.

Stasko grabs him, eliciting another yelp. Shakes him viciously. "Where's Katja? What the fuck are you playing at?"

"I don't—I can't—"

Stasko shakes him harder to get some sense out of him. Slaps him across his already-battered face.

"Where is she?!"

"I don't know who you're talking about!" the boy protests, still clutching at his leg.

"The girl! You're wearing her clothes!"

And the boy looks down, plucking at the t-shirt and leggings as if only noticing his clothing for the first time. He appears to be trying to figure out an answer to Stasko's question. Then something clicks.

"Nikolai's friend?" the boy asks.

Stasko stops shaking him. Nikolai. Bridget's guinea pig.

"Tell me where she is," he asks, more softly this time.

"I don't *know*."

"Where can I *find* her?"

"I don't *know*!" the boy pleads, then his expression suddenly changes. He points over Stasko's shoulder. "There."

Stasko looks where he is pointing, farther up the street. Sees nothing.

"Don't fuck with me. There's no one there."

The boy shakes his head wearily. Jabs his finger again. "*There*," he repeats.

"I've told you already . . ."

Stasko's words drift when he looks again. He lets go of the T-shirt, of Katja's T-shirt, and walks a few paces towards the brick wall which lines the street—towards the poster.

It's the same as the one he'd seen earlier that day, the image which instantly entranced him, except this one isn't half-torn. It is intact, including the part that had been missing from the first copy—the part which announces the time and date of the band's gig.

The Wheatsheaf. 10:00 P.M. Tonight.

Stasko checks his watch. 9:50.

He rushes back to his car, leaving the boy where he is and ignoring his pleas for help. He throws it into reverse, spins it around, once again heading in the direction was going before spotting the figure stumbling around in the darkness, when he spots Bridget's red Honda up ahead. He pulls up alongside her vehicle and she is momentarily panicked at the sudden arrival before she realizes who it is and winds down her window.

She starts to speak but Stasko cuts her off.

"I know where she is," he tells her.

28.

Frank's place, complete with a candy-cane pillar and framed portraits of long-dead models with their long-dead haircuts, is at the end of a block, separated from its neighbours by the shuttered remains of a liquor store.

DeBoer ignores the glass front entrance and walks around the back to a heavier door complete with a barred window and pornographic graffiti, the same door which he had, only a few hours earlier, been thrown out of as if he were nothing more than another piece of trash.

He knocks on the door. Waits.

Waits more.

He shifts nervously, the scratches on his arm now itching.

Maybe this isn't such a good . . .

The security plate behind the little barred window slides aside. A pair of eyes blink in the darkness.

"Frank? It's . . . it's DeBoer. I have your money."

There's a pause then the security plate slides back into place and a moment later the door is opened. Frank stands there in a dressing gown, bleary-eyed.

"I'm sorry to wake you," DeBoer says, "but I . . ."

He holds up the bags of money. "I'm here to settle up."

Frank rubs at his eyes then steps aside to let DeBoer in. He closes the door and re-engages the lock.

"Come on through," Frank says, guiding DeBoer through the shop and into what appears to be a study.

"So let's see it."

DeBoer eagerly tips the cash onto the desk before them, pushing it into neat stacks.

"It's all there," DeBoer assures him. He'd counted out the twenty thousand that he was due in the car and stuffed the rest into the remaining bag then hid it under the driver's seat, already cycling through what to do with the excess. First on the list is another poker game though he'll probably have to find somewhere else to play just in case Lady D, or some other snitch, figures out who took her money.

Frank touches the piles with one finger as if sensing the quantity by feel alone.

"So," DeBoer says, "we're all squared now?"

Frank picks up one of the bills, holds it up to the light.

"They're genuine," the detective insists, exaggerating offence. "You don't seriously think I would—"

"No," Frank says. Then he stops, the bill still pinned between two fingers. "But it looks like whoever you got it from wasn't giving it up lightly."

And he nods at the scratches on DeBoer's forearm.

29.

When Lady D comes to, the anger hits her first but it is unconnected to anything for a short time. Fizzing and hot, it dances around her like an impatient child desperate for attention. Then it snaps into place.

That pink-haired bitch Soelberg fucked her over.

She grasps at the back of her neck and finds something still sticking in there, plucks it out. An empty syringe.

Her head swims with whatever she had been injected with, muddying her thoughts and sight.

She hauls herself to her feet, struggling in her heels to right herself and having to use the alley's wall for support. She staggers around the back of the van, finds both of the rear doors wide open.

And nobody inside.

She thinks back, trying to get it all clear in her head. Watching the two women hurry away. Going to start the van, looking in the rear view mirror at the prone figure in the back. A tingling up her spine. Getting out and opening the rear door, splitting the spray-painted mouth wide. Climbing in and taking a closer look at Katja.

Not Katja.

Then a rage, calling each of the girls one by one to tell them what needs to be done, to find the nurse, and the punk, at any cost.

And then what?

She looks down at the syringe in the palm of her hand. Would Soelberg really have been stupid enough to have come back? She'd already gotten away, why risk the fight?

And then another realisation hits.

She rushes around to the driver's side, almost colliding with sheet of glass laid up against a dumpster as she continues to fight through the mental murk. The door is slightly ajar and she already knows what she will find inside.

The bags of money are gone. Her entire takings from that night—gone.

She punches the vehicle. Catches a glimpse of herself in the sideview mirror.

One side of her face is grazed and dirty. Her wig is a mess. The stolen dress is torn at the shoulder and one of her heels is damaged, hanging on by a thread. She snaps it off and throws it away.

Whoever has taken the money is dead. It's as simple as that. If it's Soelberg then she will be dead twice over— but first she needs to get a new outfit.

Lady D gets into the van, the druggy confusion respectfully fading enough to let her plan her revenge.

30.

Lady Delicious parks the van in its usual safe spot and walks the short distance home barefoot.

A combination of adrenaline and the light rain which still falls has cleared her head somewhat but also makes her more acutely aware of the aches and pains now wracking her body. She goes inside and flicks on a light. She thinks of the shower which still awaits her and is tempted to just forget about her plans for revenge but instead opts for a bottle of vodka on the kitchen counter. She downs a mouthful, stinging the grazes on the side of her mouth as some of it dribbles out but she accepts the pain, lets it revive her further.

She looks across at the guitar she'd taken from the punk earlier that day, leaning against the wall next to a potted cheese plant.

Then, still groggy from the drug, she takes the vodka with her through to her bedroom and stares at herself in the full-length mirror mounted on one wall. Shakes her head in disgust.

She opens her bag and takes out the syringe which had only minutes earlier been lodged in her neck.

She has another swig of vodka then caps the bottle and throws it onto her bed. Peels off what remains of the dress and takes off her wig. She examines the hairpiece, brushes dirt from it, de-tangling it with two fingers before placing it onto one of several polystyrene dummy heads then pulls on a dressing gown. Notices that one of her false nails is broken.

"Motherfucker," she murmurs.

She tilts her finger from side to side then looks closer. Close enough to see the scraped skin cells of her attacker buried beneath it.

"Good," she says. "I hope it fucking hurt."

She uses a cleanser to remove her makeup, stripping herself back even further, until there is nothing of Lady D left—at least not on the outside.

And now it is another reflection staring back in the mirror.

"Welcome back, Frank," he says to himself. "But I'm afraid you won't be here long."

He's about to take another swig of vodka when there's a knock at the door.

31.

So there's DeBoer on the other side of the desk, the scratches on his arm still gleaming, still a little wet. Fresh.

"They're genuine," he insists as Frank examines one of the bills. "You don't seriously think I would . . ."

"No," Frank says. Then he stops, the bill still pinned between two fingers. "But it looks like whoever you got it from wasn't giving it up lightly."

And he nods at the scratches on DeBoer's forearm.

The detective shrugs. "Nothing I can't handle."

"Clearly," Frank says.

Then reaches into his dressing gown pocket and takes out the syringe. Lays it on the table before them, on top of the cash.

DeBoer just stares at it, uncomprehending. Then he looks up and the colours drains from his face.

He doesn't say anything. He *can't* say anything.

Frank lets it all sink in a little further before sliding open the top drawer of his desk and reaching inside.

DeBoer, still frowning, still desperately catching up on what exactly is going on, raises his hands before the gun is even out.

"Oh shit, Frank, I didn't . . . I mean . . ." His words disintegrate and he shakes his head. "It can't . . . you can't . . ."

"You broke my nail," Frank says.

And shoots DeBoer.

32.

"What time is it?" Katja asks.

They push their way through the crowds coming out of the small movie theatre they have been holed up in ever since splitting from Nikolai's squat.

"Coming on for ten," he tells her. "How far is it from here?"

"Not far," she says, quickening her pace. She feels more secure in the baggy clothes but at the same time ridiculous, not at all herself. She has the top zipped as far as it will go and the hood pulled up, her head dipped and her hands in her pockets. She walks as quickly as she dares to without drawing attention.

Nikolai tries to keep up.

"Are you sure you want to do this?"

"Stop asking me that," she says as they leave the crowds behind. "Look, I'm just going to get the gig done, get the money, pay *your fucking debt* then . . ."

Then what?

She isn't thinking that far ahead.

"It's just up ahead," she says, changing the subject.

They cross the street, the traffic light but the rain now heavy, and hurry towards a building isolated from those around it by plastic barriers. Scaffolding climbs up the building's walls like metallic vines, the brickwork charred, the posters which had once adorned it now burned and peeling and pasted over with warning signs.

Outside is a small group of bikers, their rides parked on the street, and an even smaller group of teenage girls, designer stockings tattooing their skinny legs with spiderwebs and dizzying patterns. The girls pass a cigarette between one another, flirting with the bouncer, and neither they nor the bikers look up as Katja and Nikolai pass.

"Hey."

They both freeze.

"You two."

Katja turns to see the bouncer coming towards them.

Nikolai leans in, whispers "What do we—"

"Just shut up," Katja whispers back. Then, to the bouncer, "Yeah?"

"Hood down," he says, his hands still firmly planted in his bomber jacket's pockets, jaw working on a piece of chewing gum.

Katja takes her hood down. The bouncer looks from her to the poster on the wall behind her, the one which is repeated all over the entrance.

"You're late," he says.

"Then we can go?"

But he's already walking back towards the teenage girls.

As the two go into the club the city outside is crushed beneath the noise of the chatter of the crowds within as well as The Broken's warm-up act: a four piece called Damage Sticks who look like they have been dug up from their graves and dusted off before being thrown on stage. Their set comes to an end, feedback ringing out over a smattering of applause and cheers.

Katja and Nikolai go around the back of the stage, a roadie about to get in their way before recognising Katja and letting them through. She leads Nikolai into the rear corridor where the rest of the band are already gathered.

"Where the fuck have you been?!" Joey shouts when he sees her.

"We're due on in about five minutes," Max adds as he slings the bass guitar around his chunky neck.

"I got here as quick as I could," Katja says. "Had some stuff to deal with."

"What, and it couldn't wait?" And it's only then that Joey realizes who she has brought with her.

"Well look who's crawled out from under his rock."

Nikolai remains behind Katja, head dipped.

"What the fuck is he doing here?"

"There's your answer," Katja says and nods past them.

Max and Joey turn to see three figures at the other end of the corridor, silhouetted by the green light of the exit sign above them. All that can readily be made out are the extravagant beehives which each one of them wears.

The three approach, each strike of their heels like a bullet being fired.

"You're here," Lady D, in the middle of the other two

and wearing a skimpy leopard print number, says. "I'm impressed."

She motions to one of her heavies who duly produces Katja's guitar from behind their back, holding it up by the neck.

Katja looks at Lady D who raises her chin in consent then Katja takes the instrument.

"Now go do your thing and we can put this all to bed," Lady D tells her, glossy pink lips tweaked into a smile "There's a hot shower waiting for me and I'm not about to put it off any longer."

"What's going on, Katja?" Max asks. Joey remains silent, having backed away a few paces.

"Nothing," Katja says, maintaining eye contact with Lady D.

Over the speakers comes the sound of Dimebag Dexter attempting to generate some applause for Damage Sticks, then starting his disinterested spiel about The Broken.

"It's my fault," Nikolai says, stepping out from behind Katja. His hands are clenched into fists at his side. "The debt is mine. I should . . . it's up to me to pay."

Lady D frowns, her hands on her hips. "I'm sorry, and you are?"

Now it's Nikolai's turn to be confused. "Uhhh . . . Nikolai?"

As if he's making a guess.

"You trying to fuck with me?" Lady D asks, her tone darkening as her attention goes from Nikolai to Katja and back.

"I . . . no . . . I just . . . the debt . . . the debt's mine. I'm the one who came to you in the first place. Wasn't I?"

"Look, this has been a *fucking* long night so if you think you can all worm your way out of this then I can assure you I am in no mood to be played with. Whatever you think you're achieving by covering for your little friend over there it isn't going to work."

And she points at Joey, who is quietly backing away. He stops when they all look at him.

"What's Joey got to do with any of this?" Katja asks.

"*Joey?*" Lady D parrots, her tone disdainful. "I've already told you, don't try playing games with me."

"What the hell are you talking you about?"

Lady D lets out a sharp, irritated grunt. "That's *Nikolai*," she says, pointing again at Joey. "That's the one who took out the loan."

33.

"Hey, Nikolai, wait," Joey says, jogging to catch up with the other man as he walks away from the small outcrop of run-down shed-style buildings. "You guys rehearsing again?"

"Uh, yeah," Nikolai tells him without slowing his pace.

"Cool. You okay if I hang out again?"

"I don't . . . didn't Katja say she'd prefer it if you just stuck to the gigs?"

"Nah, you must have mis-heard," Joey says. "Anyway, you ain't done any gigs yet."

"Soon," Nikolai tells him. "Katja's already sorting something out."

"Yeah I know, she told me."

"She told you," Nikolai repeats. He crosses the street abruptly but Joey sticks close to him.

"Well, I overheard her telling *you*, more precisely," Joey corrects himself. "Man, you guys are going to fucking *kill* when the times come though. Still reckon you could do with another guitarist though. Or another drummer."

And he slaps Nikolai playfully across the shoulders.

"I think she wants to keep it tight," Nikolai tells him. "But I'm sure if we ever need anyone . . ."

The sentiment drifts and his pace quickens again. Joey matches it.

"I'm just ribbin' you, man," Joey says. "Don't even worry about it. I mean, I can play, sure, but not like you. So what you practising tonight? Anything new?"

"I don't know," Nikolai tells him. "Look, tonight, I don't even know if we're hooking up to play, we might just be talking about the first gigs and . . ."

"That's fine, that's totally fine by me," Joey says.

They come the end of the block, the sidewalk crumbling into chunks of concrete and stone as if some creature from a *daikaiju* movie had stomped on it and destroyed whatever had been there before. The road fades into scruffy turf which leads towards a series of single-storey buildings in the near distance and from them is the muffled sound of guitar noise. The only other sign of life nearby is a takeaway van, the owner scrubbing at the folded-down service area with a grubby cloth.

Nikolai stops. "Seriously, Joey, there's really not going to be that much going on tonight."

Joey looks at him then nods. "Okay. Okay, sure. Then at least let me buy you a coffee before you start. Just in case the session turns epic?"

Nikolai shakes his head. "I don't think—"

"Hey, man, I know you're trying to get clean but I didn't realize it extended to coffee," Joey jokes.

"I *am* clean," Nikolai corrects him.

"Sure, of course, that's what I meant. But Katja's not

going to kick you out of the band because of a little caffeine is she? And you're probably needing your hits from wherever you can get them now, right?"

Nikolai sighs, finally gives into Joey's persistence. "Okay," he says.

"Cool, you just go on ahead, I'll grab them and catch up. I won't stay if you guys need peace though—as long as you promise to let me sit in on the next session?"

"Fine," Nikolai says, already walking away.

"Great," Joey says then crosses to the takeaway van. He orders two coffees which the owner promptly delivers.

"Sugar and shit are over there," the man says, indicating a series of plastic tubs at the far end of the service hatch then going back to his surface-wiping.

Joey puts the two cups down next to the tubs. He spoons a couple of sugars into each, a little UHT milk from an already-open container. Then he reaches into his pocket and takes out a little plastic bag of pills. He checks the man is still cleaning then drops two of the pills into one of the coffees. Then drops another two in. Then empties the bag into it. He stirs the coffee until the spoon no longer collides with the solid mass of the pills, then snaps on one of the lids stacked in a neat pile to one side.

He thanks the man and walks across the scrub-land towards the row of shacks and the sound of discordant punk music.

34.

Joey is backed into the doorway of a storage cupboard, Katja and Nikolai on one side, Lady D and her crew on the other.

"Come on, Katja," he protests. "You know as well as anyone, once a useless junkie, always a useless junkie. He was bound to fuck up at some point. Better that it happened before you got any gigs organised."

"I always knew you were a snidey little piece of shit," she says. "I just never realized it was to this extent."

"Don't put this on me, I did you a favour."

"Then let me do you one," she tells him and swings the guitar at him.

It smashes into his head, throwing him back against the doorway and he bounces against the frames for a second or two before slumping to the ground.

It's only then that they become aware of the shouts and chants of the restless crowd. A moment later Dimebag Dexter appears, flustered and sweaty.

"What the shitting hell is going on back here, I've been calling you for . . ." He stops when he sees Joey's body, slumped and bloody. "What the . . . ? Do we have a problem here?"

"No problem," Katja says quickly. "Just a little . . . disagreement."

"Not the sort of disagreement which means that you aren't about to get up there and play, I hope," Dexter threatens. "Because if it *is* that sort then you are going to be in some serious bloody—"

"It's fine," Katja tells him. "Nik, grab his sticks."

"His what?" Nikolai says, still taking it all in.

"His *sticks*," Katja repeats.

Nikolai reaches down and slides the drumsticks from Joey's slack hands. A single droplet of blood glistens on the tip of one of them.

"And who the hell are you?" Dexter asks. "The manager?"

Lady D crosses her arms, straightening herself so that she gains yet another inch over the little man. The two on either side of her do the same.

"Of a sort," she tells him, her nostrils flaring. "I'm here to collect their fee."

"Yeah, well, I got your money right here," he tells her, slapping at his jacket, "and that's where it's going to stay—until you lot get out there and do what I hired you to do. You've got precisely one minute."

And he storms off again, clearing the way for them to reach the stage. The crowd is booing now and there's the occasional explosion of a bottle smashing against a wall.

"Well?" Katja says once he's gone.

"Well what?" Lady D replies.

"The debt. It was never ours in the first place. This little fuckwit . . ."

"Took it out in the name of the band. Whoever he is—at this point I really do not care. Nothing has changed. The debt stands."

"And she always collects," one of the cross-dressing thugs adds proudly.

"The crowd are waiting," Lady D says, using her glittery clutch bag to wave them on.

"Fine," Katja says, slipping her guitar back on. "Let's get this done."

35.

The crowd milling around outside looks like the result of an explosion in a leather and metal factory. They flash and sparkle as they move beneath the lights of the Wheatsheaf's shaky-looking entrance, the smoke from their cigarettes curling around proud mohawks and gleaming liberty spikes.

Bridget stops in her tracks, looks up at the scaffold-clad building suspiciously, subconsciously adjusting the fresh pair of gloves she has pulled on.

"Is this place safe?" she asks Stasko, standing beside her.

Steel struts and joists are bolted to the cracked exterior, fresh cement smeared around them. Ribbons of safety tape flap in the breeze.

Stasko ignores her concerns and hands the doorman enough money to cover their entrance then places a hand on the small of Bridget's back and guides her inside. She feels a sudden claustrophobic panic as she is led into the darkened corridor beyond, a wall of noise tumbling up the passageway like a marauding beast, and she has to fight to keep the fear of Stasko knowing about what she has done that night in check.

They emerge into the performance area, noticing the empty stage at the rear of the room. Stasko continues to push her forward as if he's a prison guard leading her back to her cell, navigating around the back of the crowds, past the bar and towards a pillar near the stage. A large piece of fabric hand-painted with the words *Damage Sticks* written across it is pulled down by a roadie. He bundles it up, throws it behind one of the immense speakers beside him, then sets to work rearranging the drum kit.

"What now?" Bridget asks but gets no response. She realizes that Stasko hasn't heard her, her voice drowned out by the static-laden rock music being blasted over the loudspeakers. For a brief instant she considers slipping into the crowd, of losing him long enough to make her escape, but the thought falls apart when she thinks about what she'd do next. No, for now at least, she'll need to play along.

She leans into him, cups her hand around his ear and repeats the question.

He returns the gesture to reply but his words are lost as the crowd suddenly roars and he abandons the response. Hands are raised and people start jumping up and down.

Bridget struggles to see past them but can just make out figures emerging onto the stage. There's a crackling fizz of static as instruments are plugged in, a short burst of drumming and a couple of notes struck. The music being played over the loudspeakers fades out. The crowd shuffles as some push nearer and others prepare for a mosh pit, stripping off their shirts.

From somewhere off-stage the name of The Broken is announced with resounding disinterest and finally Bridget spots Katja as she steps up to the mike. The punk unzips the over-sized hoodie she wears and drops it to the ground, revealing a tight black top beneath from under which her neck tattoo emerges. Self-consciously, Bridget touches a hand to the side of her head where she had been struck and where it is still tender. But she's not here for revenge, she doesn't care about Katja one way or another.

Unlike Stasko.

As the first chords ring out Bridget can see how entranced he is, his mouth slightly open and his eyes wide. She recognises that look from the clinic, from him pouring over designs and photographs for one of those who has come to him for a secret treatment.

She's pushed to one side by someone near to her, catches herself against the column and feels it shiver. She looks up, following the line of the concrete up towards the ceiling and notices more scaffold up there in the darkness.

Stasko nudges her and nods towards the stage then leans in towards her. "The drummer," he shouts at her.

She follows his gaze between the bouncing, spike-haired heads in front of her, until she spots the man sitting at the drum kit.

The guinea pig. Nikolai.

She looks back at Stasko but he isn't particularly bothered by the recognition, merely interested. His attention is already back to Katja.

She cups her hand around his ear once more and repeats her earlier question. "What do we do now?"

"We wait," he shouts and this time she hears him.

He moves in front of her to get a better view whilst still remaining behind a large skinhead just in case Katja were to spot him and again Bridget has to suppress her desire to run. She looks around, at least wanting to know where the exits are in case she should need them.

And that's when she spots the transvestite.

36.

In the crowd, Lady D can see the bobbing beehives of her girls, precisely positioned at each corner of the club. Despite her grudging respect for the fact that Katja has actually made it to the venue and is going through with the gig she isn't about to assume that the girl has no more tricks up her sleeves and so isn't taking any chances.

She's standing on the small set of steps which lead up to the stage, away from the main crowds but closer to one of the stacked speakers than she is comfortable with. She pins a finger in each ear as the song's intensity grows, watching the drummer, the *real* Nikolai, as it turns out, slamming away at the kit. The drowsy nervousness that had been there earlier is now gone, replaced by determination and focus. The bass guitarist has his head tipped back, his jaw jutting out proudly, head nodding into time to Nikolai's beat.

Meanwhile Katja barks and screams into the microphone before breaking away and thrashing at her guitar with a series of chuggy chords, slamming it against her thigh and pulling it around as if she were wrestling it rather than playing it. Even from this distance and in the low light of the club Lady D can see how the girl's eyes glisten with pleasure, how they sparkle with a life that hadn't been there previously. It's the same look Lady D sees in her own eyes once she has doused herself in her makeup and put on her heels, her fake breasts, and her gaff.

The girl's energy floods out across the crowds, feeding them, and despite the awful noise, even Lady D can't help but smile.

The first song ends and there is a smattering of applause amongst those who are sober enough to notice. The debt collector ducks as a couple of plastic beer cups are thrown at the stage, what remains of their contents sprayed around.

It's when she stands back upright that she spots the woman in the crowd, lurking by one of the concrete pillars near the stage, her stiff, unmoving posture in stark contrast to the jittering movements around her. The one who had dumped her with the fake. The CCTV freak.

Soelberg.

"Well, well," Lady D says to herself, though the words are muffled beneath the ringing in her ears.

She catches the attention of Patty, eyeing up a beefy biker who has stripped to the waist as he orders more beers, then motions towards the woman. Patty pushes herself up onto her tip-toes, locating what Lady D is indicating. She mouths the word: *Pinky?*

Lady D nods, mouths in return: *I want her.*

Patty gives her a thumbs-up then vanishes into the crowd.

Nikolai's drums tap out the intro to the next song. Lady D finds Lucille at the other end of the club and motions for her to cover the exit. The bass guitar kicks in.

Lady D steps down into the crowd, giving up her vantage point and having to push her weight through the sweaty, beery bodies. One man refuses to move when he sees her, leering then reaching out for her breasts. On another night she might have broken his arm but right now she doesn't have time for it, instead snatching his wrist and pulling him towards her then slamming her forehead into his nose. He drops as Katja's guitar joins in, matching the notes of the bass, and he crashes to the ground before being swallowed up by the crowd.

Lady D continues to push her way through, circling around so that she might get closer to the woman without being seen when she is suddenly shoved from behind. She tumbles forwards, splitting a group of teenagers huddled together around a shared beer, and before she knows it she is only a few feet away from her target.

Soelberg spots Lady D and panic fills her eyes. She starts to turn then finds Patty, resplendent in a gold lamé dress and matching heels, standing right beside her. Soelberg looks back at Lady D. Lady D raises one finger and waggles it from side to side.

Naughty naughty.

Patty grabs her.

37.

Stasko is only vaguely aware of being pushed from one side to the other, of being shoved in the back and elbowed and shouted at by the crowd around him. Even the raucous music fades to a background drone. All he sees is Katja.

The stage lights flash from green to red to blue and back again, flaring and exploding, variously illuminating the beads of perspiration that glisten on the girl. She screams into the microphone, the guitar hanging loose around her neck, both hands clutching it. He studies her exquisite architecture, watching the way her jawbone flexes and her forehead creases. Sweat pools in the pit of her neck, describing the outline of the tracheostomy tube which he had fitted there only a short while earlier, surrounded by her tattoo as if it were all part of some fine art installation. He watches the muscles in her upper arms flex as she goes back to thrashing the guitar, the curve of her spine when she turns around.

The circle pit in front of him widens and he has to take a step back to avoid being dragged into it. He collides with someone, spinning him sideways, crashing him into another group of teens. The bottle that one of them is holding shatters on the ground and he angrily shoves Stasko back in the direction he came, the word *asshole* forming inaudibly on the lips of the girl beside him. Stasko reaches out a hand and steadies himself against a supporting column then looks up and the stage is gone, replaced by the bar. He struggles for his bearing for several moments, but just before he is about to turn to face the front again he sees Bridget—just as a pair of thick, hairy arms reach out for her.

She's too busy looking in the other direction, transfixed by something, her eyes wide with terror and she's grabbed before she knows what's going on. Her attacker leans forward and the arms belong not to a biker but to a transvestite wearing a sparkling gold lamé dress and cherry red lipstick. Bridget cries out, the sound lost beneath the chaotic thrash blaring through the amps, but her eyes meet Stasko's. She reaches out for him over the shoulder of her cross-dressing abductor.

Stasko pushes through the crowd towards her and collides once more with the group of teenagers. This time instead of shoving him back one of them grabs him by the collar and swings a fierce punch at his head. Stasko pulls away and the punch sails wide, connecting with a Hispanic man with a purple mohawk and a neck like a tree root. The man pounces onto the teenager as Stasko pushes past, keeping Bridget in sight as she is dragged into the crowd, but then another punch is thrown and an elbow connects with his temple.

There is angry jeering and a bottle smashes, then another. Stasko tries to break through, Bridget and the

Tgirl nowhere to be seen. He shouts her name then as he ducks another punch, the entire crowd around him now engaged in an exchange of blows. Someone picks up a dropped bottle and throws it at the stage and Stasko watches it sail through the air and smash into the bass player's head.

38.

As she sings the final verse Katja becomes aware of a sudden explosion of movement in the crowd to her right, something which goes beyond the usual mosh pit antics. An instant later something flies through the air towards them and then there's an audible *thunk* as it hits Max. The bassline drops out and he sways from side to side, grabs a stack amp next to him to stop himself from falling over.

Katja looks into the crowd and spots the one who threw it, fists raised in celebration as fights continue to break out around him.

Without missing a beat Katja takes two steps and throws herself from the stage, diving over the crowd and at the man. Those at the front reach up and grab her, unaware of the chaos going on behind them, pushing her backwards to let her crowd surf. Her amp lead snaps out of its socket so only Nikolai's drums remain.

The one who threw the bottle's expression changes when he sees her coming, just a moment before she lashes out with the guitar and connects fully with his forehead.

The crowd drops her and she crashes to the ground next to the man she just attacked, his eyes rolled back into their sockets and his fists still clenched in the ghost of celebration. She quickly gets to her feet, hands grabbing at her as she pushes her way back towards the front.

A couple of bouncers part the crowd for her and haul her back up onto the stage, more to remove another potential source of trouble than through any concern for her safety, and not before one of them delivers a quick knee to her face. She crawls the rest of the way, blood dribbling from a split lip and Nikolai looks up in confusion, as if only just noticing that the rest of his band has stopped playing. Beside her, Max is slowly getting to his feet, blood trickling from a nasty gash in the side of his head.

Katja reaches down to plug her guitar back in and something sails overhead, something which makes a *whooshing* noise as it goes. It smashes into the wall behind Nikolai and bursts into flames, leaving a trail of fire rolling down the brickwork. Katja turns back to the crowd, half of it charging towards the exit, the other half busy punching and kicking the living shit out of each other. She snaps the guitar lead back into place and the amps start to buzz with her feedback once more.

She strikes a power cord, motioning for Nikolai to pick up the beat again. She looks at Max, now on his feet but pulling the bass from around his neck. She walks to him, shouts, *"What the fuck are you doing?"*

"Getting the hell out of here!" he shouts back, then holds up his hand to show her the blood from his head wound.

Katja bares her teeth, stained red from her split lip.

"*What for?!*"

"*What for? Look the fuck around, Katja!*"

Another bottle smashes into the amps beside them, this one thankfully lacking an ignition source.

"*It's a little bit lively, that's all!*" she shouts back, thrashing another chord and letting it ring out.

He shakes his head then throws the bass to the ground and stalks past her across the stage—stops suddenly and looks up.

Beneath the hum of Katja's power chord and the chaotic shouts of the crowd there is another sound—a low, ominous creak. Katja follows his gaze towards the temporary steel beams which criss-cross the Wheatsheaf's ceiling.

It looks as if they're moving.

"Oh shit . . ."

39.

With the sudden eruption of violence around her, Lady D is carried backwards by the crowd, away from Patty and from Soelberg. She fights her way back through but time and again has to duck away from a wayward punches and before she knows what is happening she finds herself next to the stage.

Lady D pulls herself up onto the rear of the stage, lashing out with a heeled foot when one of the roadies grabs her, and gets to her feet. She surveys the room, searching for Patty or Soelberg but instead notices the club's owner hurrying away down the rear corridor.

"No you don't," Lady D says to herself and then charges after him. Something sails through the air and crashes into the wall behind her and, glancing back, she sees flames are spilling down to the ground.

Ignoring them she hurries down the corridor as the man struggles to open the locking bar to the emergency exit door. He sees her coming and his attempts become more frantic until finally the latch releases and the door swings open. Before he can escape, however, Lady D lands a hefty punch to the back of his neck. He's thrown forwards and slams into the door, rebounding off of it and back towards the debt collector. She is ready for him, stepping to one side to let him stagger past just enough to deliver another blow.

He slumps to the ground and she reaches into the coat pocket he had earlier patted when confirming he had the gig fee. She smiles as she touches the wad of cash and pulls it out. She thumbs it quickly to check the full amount then kneels next to the man.

He groans softly when she strokes his head.

"I always get my money, sweetheart," she says, then stands up.

Lady D retrieves her clutch bag from the spare mike stand she had hung it on before the gig and stuffs the cash inside. For a moment she hesitates, deciding whether to go back to see if Patty still has Soelberg or whether it even matters now she has her money, and it's as she is still mulling the decision over that she becomes aware of the creaking noises.

She ducks her head out of the corridor, back into the gig-come-riot, noticing the flames which are now spreading around the rear of the stage and climbing up to the ceiling, to the patchwork of beams that are supporting the place's roof, beams which look as if they are beginning to bend.

And she realizes that the place's owner wasn't just escaping to keep a hold of his money.

"Oh shit . . ."

40.

The punches stop flying.

The music is gone.

Stasko is let go by the skinhead who had a hold of him and he follows his attacker's gaze upwards.

"Oh shit . . ."

41.

Bridget is shoved out of the crowd and towards the bar and crashes into the counter, the Tgirl still with a fistful of her bright pink hair. Bridget closes her eyes and braces herself for another series of blows but instead is dropped to the ground when the debt collector's grip is released.

High above, the sound of metal rending. Bridget opens her eyes.

"Oh shit . . ."

42.

As Katja comes to, a vicious blast of fluorescent light floods in and her nostrils flare with the stench of disinfectant. She blinks and lifts her head enough to realize where she is.

A hospital bed.

A split second after the realisation hits she panics, certain that the mad surgeon has once again captured her, her thoughts swirl in a mist of confusion as she tries to recall if she had ever actually escaped. Then she thinks of Nikolai. Of the squat and the pink-haired nurse.

And the gig.

The building caving in on itself.

She groans as her brain slowly sparks back into life, bringing with it an array of pain signals from nerve endings all across her body. Her throat and chest burn as she breathes in and she starts to cough. An almost deafening ringing fills her ears.

Someone touches her arm and her hand is already balled into a fist before she recognises Nikolai.

"Wait!" he protests.

He's standing beside the bed, his skin covered in a coating of sweat and dirt and one side of his face darkened with bruising, a deep cut at the centre of it. He puts a finger to his lips to quiet her. Katja's vision finally clearing, she looks around and she's not back in the surgeon's dungeon—it's an ER.

Doctors and nurses scuttle around, dragging IV units and portable defibrillators behind them, calling to one another in that strange abbreviated language they share. The ward is lined with beds, some with curtains drawn around them, others revealing bloodied, battered bodies draped across them. Announcements crackle over the PA system in a constant stream and people are herded from place to place.

"Can you hear me? Look at me, Katja."

She blinks again, his words muffled by the ringing in her ears.

"We have to get out of here."

She waves him away, still trying to clear her head, trying to make sense of it all. Looking down at herself, she sees that she is covered in the same grime as Nikolai, her clothes singed and grubby. They all are. She swings her legs across the bed and almost loses her balance, slumping towards the floor. Nikolai catches and holds her until she is steady.

"Are you okay? Are you hurt?"

The truth is she doesn't know. She eases herself away from him, waiting for new pain to shoot up her legs or back, but nothing comes. There is just the background buzz of the ache which envelopes her.

"I'm okay," she says finally, doing her best to look it and failing miserably. She waggles an index finger in each ear as she could knock the ringing sound loose.

"We need to go—the Policie are on their way and fuck knows who else . . ."

She stumbles past him before he can finish the sentence, tugging an IV line from one arm. He tries to put an arm around her for support but she pushes him away.

"Which way?"

He points towards a large desk at the opposite side of the room, almost lost behind the mass of bodies. More gurneys are being wheeled in, the devices and their inhabitants abandoned wherever there is space. Together they negotiate their way through it all until Katja stops suddenly.

"What is it?"

She looks down at a gurney, a sheet pulled up over the body laid on it and a dark patch of blood staining one side. Sticking out of the end of the sheet are a pair of large feet cradled in six-inch heels and attached to one of the heels is an identification tag. The name *Jane Doe* has been written on it then crossed out and replaced with *John Doe*.

"That's one way to get her off our back," Katja says.

There's a burst of activity nearby and the two duck back against the wall as another body is wheeled through, one badly burned arm reaching out aimlessly, desperate for any sort of help.

"Come on," Nikolai says, pulling her after him.

"Wait," she says. "My guitar."

"What?"

"My *guitar*," she repeats. "Before the roof came down . . . I still had it on me."

"So?"

"*So* I'm pretty sure we're not going to be seeing the gig fee any time soon and I didn't bring the fucking thing all the way from the island and spend what little cash I had getting it fixed up just so some thieving paramedic could keep it for himself!" she says.

She snatches her arm away from him and stalks past Lady D's body back to the bed she had awoken in. She pulls open the door of the small unit next to the bed but it's empty. She then checks under the bed and behind it.

"They put it all in a safe room," Nikolai says. "Personal belongings I mean. Whenever there's a big incident like this and a sudden influx of people they don't have time to sort out all the possessions so they just bag it up and stick it in a safe room."

Katja stops and looks up at him.

He shrugs. "I spend a lot of time in hospitals. You pick these things up."

"Uh-huh. And you know where this safe room is?"

"Yeah. I'm pretty sure."

She holds up her arms in exasperation when he says nothing further.

"Well let's go find it so we can get the fuck out of here!"

43.

They hide around the corner from the room Nikolai had identified moments earlier, just long enough to see a nurse unlocking the padlocked door. He drops the green plastic bag he holds into the room then closes the door, snapping the padlock shut before rushing back into the ER.

As soon as he is gone the two cross to the door, attempting to look inconspicuous. When she is sure nobody is looking Katja tries the padlock on the off-chance the nurse had been in too much of a rush to close it properly.

No such luck.

"Let me," Nikolai says and she turns to find him standing next to her, unwrapping a scalpel still sealed in its sterile packet. He tears into another packet and takes out another tool, this one with a narrow hook on the end.

"Where did you . . . ?"

Nikolai nods at an instrument trolley a few metres away then goes to work on the padlock. Katja hurriedly positions herself in front of him, nervously watching the people rushing back and forth past them, spotting the a pair of Policie officers in their distinctive dogwitch-black uniforms at the end of the corridor.

"Policie are here," she says without looking at him. "Hurry up."

And as if on cue the lock clicks. Nikolai opens the door and lets her in, coming in behind her and closing the door again. He reaches for the light switch but Katja stops him.

"Wait," she whispers.

Together they listen to the sound of four heavily booted feet stomping towards them, Katja's shoulder pressed against the door just in case the Policie had spotted them and were going to barge in.

"You still have that scalpel?" she asks, again in a whisper. She sees a glint of light as Nikolai holds it up.

The footsteps grow louder. Louder.

Then pass by and are swallowed up by the sounds of the ER.

Katja flicks the light switch to illuminate the room. Nikolai stands next to her, the sweat rolling down his face mixing with blood from his wound and turning pink where it collects along his jaw. He's still holding the instruments in his hand.

"You and locks, huh?" she says.

Then turns to the piles of plastic bags, all the same green colour as the one they had seen the nurse dropping in. Each one is held shut by little metal-lined ties of the sort you would normally seal a sandwich bag with and each one has a label attached to it, pierced by the tie. On the labels are names or physical descriptions.

None are big enough to contain her guitar and so she pushes them to one side, revealing other, larger items lain out beneath them or stacked against the wall behind them.

"Hurry," Nikolai says. "I think I hear more Policie."

Katja mutters something then cries out. "Got it!" she shouts, and pushes aside more bags. She climbs over more bags to reach the instrument, grabbing it by the neck and pulling it free. She examines it quickly. It's covered in a layer of grimy soot and scorched in one corner near the base, the paint there cracked and curling but aside from that and some snapped strings it's in a pretty decent condition.

"What's that?" she asks when she sees that Nikolai is looking down at one of the plastic bags.

This one hasn't been sealed properly and lies open, revealing the glittery clutch bag within. Nikola reaches inside and takes it out then looks to Katja who nods for him to continue. He pops open the clip that holds the bag shut.

"Hello there," Katja says when the wad of cash inside is revealed.

"You think it's the gig money?"

"Does it matter? From the look of her out there I don't think she's going to be making much use of it anymore do you? Anyway the debt wasn't even ours in the first place. Right?"

Despite her assertions they both continue to stare at the money as if it is somehow cursed. Finally Katja snatches it and stuffs it into the pockets of her oversized trousers before she can change her mind. Then she picks up the guitar by its neck and flicks off the light switch. She listens though the door before opening it barely an inch and peering through the gap.

"Okay," she says, stepping out into the corridor. Nikolai closes the door behind them.

Katja takes a moment to regain her bearings then starts back up the corridor again, dissolving into the human traffic and heading for the exit, her guitar in one hand, the money in her pockets.

The crowds thin and they reach a junction. There's a sudden burst of static from around the corner and the two of them freeze.

And a moment later a single Policie officer, one hand clamped over the radio strapped to his shoulder in an attempt to muffle it, steps into view.

44.

Lady D sits upright, an alarm of some kind going off nearby, and for a few moments she's reaching around blindly to switch it off before realising that she isn't in her own bed—or even her own home.

A nurse charges past her, grabbing the plastic curtain which hangs from the rail of the bed next to her and pulling it around as the figure lying on the bed thrashes around. Through the curtain Lady D can see the bleary outline of several figures tending to the patient before the alarm goes silent.

She flips away the thin sheet which has been spread over her, rubbing her head to clear it. Swings her legs off the side of the bed, watching the medical staff rush back and forth between the beds which line the room. In the middle is a circular reception desk, and only the top of the head of the person sitting at it is visible. A large whiteboard is suspended from the false ceiling above, names and numbers hastily scribbled across it in different coloured inks.

She stands up, assesses herself. Her muscles are stiff and her left arm throbs with a deep ache and her skin is covered in an oily grime which won't come off no matter how much she rubs it but compared to most of the others she can see in the emergency room, she's gotten off lightly.

Lady D runs a hands across her head and is appalled to find her wig gone, suddenly feeling exposed. Her dress is torn at the hem and stained with the same oily residue yet otherwise fine but she can't find her heels. She attempts to get everything clear in her head and remembers the gig, then spotting the nurse, Soelberg, in the crowd. Going after her. Then . . .

She looks up the ceiling, momentarily blinded by the fluorescent lights.

Her bag.

The memory of taking the money from Dimebag Dexter and stuffing it into her clutch bag unfolds itself and the panic returns.

She blinks away the purple-red cloud which fogs her vision then searches around the bed, the checks inside the plastic-coated cabinet next to the bed. She lifts the mattress, checks the end of the bed in case it is hanging there. Nothing.

She grabs a young doctor as he strides past, snatching his coat by the sleeve.

"Where's my stuff?"

His eyes are wide with fear at the sight of her and he attempts to form a response but none comes.

She jerks him closer, close enough that he'll be able to see the fine grains of stubble beginning to emerge along her jawline. "I want my stuff."

"It's . . . you'll have to ask at reception," he tells her.

"Any valuables—"

She pushes him away, letting him stumble into a crash-cart, then crosses barefoot to the circular desk in the middle of the ER. A pair of Slavic-looking women shove themselves back and forth on wheeled stools, going from phones to computers and back again, being shouted at by the doctors and shouting back. One of them spins around and scribbles on the board suspended in the air behind them, adding a series of indecipherable symbols next to one of the many names written on it. When she turns back Lady D is leaning over the counter towards her.

"I want my stuff," she says.

A nurse calls across and the woman waves an acknowledgement to them. "I'm sorry," she says in a thick accent. "You need to excuse us, we very busy."

"Then tell me where my stuff is and I'll get out of your way."

"Personal belongings in secure room, they—" She turns away, shouts something to the other receptionist who has just rushed to hand one of the doctors a small stack of papers.

"Where is the room?"

The woman grimaces, sweeps a hand across her forehead to clear sweat-clotted strands of hair. "In the *secure* room," she insists, briefly pointing towards one of two corridors which lead out of the ER. "You'll have to put in a request but I don't think we—"

"I'm *putting* in a request," Lady D says, leaning in a little closer. "This is my request."

The woman shakes her head, retrieves a pink form and hands it to her. "This is the form. You fill this out and wait. Someone will get your things for you. Please, we're very busy."

The phone goes and she picks it up, turning away and scoring out a couple of names on the whiteboard. Lady D waits a couple of moments then stalks away, across the ER and into the corridor the woman had indicated. It's quieter than the chaos of the ER but there is still a steady stream of people. She finds the door that the receptionist pointed to and sees that it is padlocked. She cups a hand to her eyes and peers in through the little window adjacent but the blinds drawn across it afford her little view.

She becomes aware of an elderly man watching her, gnarled hands gripping a walking stick in front of him.

"You stare any longer and I'm going to have to start charging you, honey," she snaps and he shuffles off, muttering to himself.

She tries the padlock and is surprised to find that it isn't actually locked. The curved metal peg is in position but hasn't been fully clicked into place. She pulls it out of the handle and opens the door, steps inside. She flicks a switch and a single light blinks into life, illuminating the mass of green plastic bags stacked against one another. Some are upturned and emptied, their contents strewn across the floor.

Someone has beaten her to it.

She grabs bags at random, instantly discarding those which are too heavy or too light to be her belongings, noticing that each one has a tag tied to it with either a name or a description on it. She tears open a couple of them and empties out their contents, kicking the items across the floor in frustration.

Then she spots another bag, this one also torn open and with its tag still attached. She bends down and picks it up, reads it.

~~Female~~ *Male \ 6' \ dark shaven hair (cheap blonde wig) \ Leopard print dress. Items: clutch bag, wig.*

"Cheap?" she says angrily, then checks the torn bag to make sure it is empty. She throws it across the room in disgust. Someone *has* beaten her to it.

This, she realizes, is the point where most collectors will give up and decide that the money isn't worth it . So this, she knows, is exactly the point at which she will *not* give up.

She scans the room, looking for any clue as to who had gotten there before her, and quickly spots another tag and bag. This time the bag isn't torn but instead twisted, as if it has been wrapped around something. She checks the tag. Again no name, just a description.

Female \ 5'5" \ shaved head \ multiple tattoos. Items: guitar.

Lady D crumples the tag as her hand becomes a fist. She stands up, rage boiling inside her now. It's only when she uncurls her fingers that she notices the blood drops which stain the tag, then another couple of splashes on the floor. She touches one of them with a toe. Still tacky.

She drops the bag and leaves the room, not bothering to shut the door behind her, not caring if anyone saw her. Instead she looks for any more drops of blood and finds them, a little trail which leads into the corridor, most of them smeared by footfalls.

An orderly wheels a gurney towards her, shoving it up against a wall then rushing back into ER. A pair of shiny gold lamé heels stick out from beneath the bloody sheet which covers the body laid out beneath it.

"It's what you would have wanted, Patty," she says, taking them then stroking one of the corpse's ice-cold feet.

She slips the shoes on, an almost-perfect fit, then follows the trail of blood drops up the corridor and around a corner into a farther, quieter passageway.

Smiling to herself now.

Knowing that she is going to get her money back, no matter what.

She follows the blood drops.

45.

"Normally we'd get someone to take you to the exit but under the current circumstances . . ."

"It's fine," Stasko tells the young doctor, waving him away. The man helps Stasko from the bed and to his feet, the scent of the antiseptic they had doused his wounds in clouding around him.

"The injuries are minor but should you feel any drowsiness or neck pains, please come straight back."

Stasko nods as much as his stiff neck allows. His left side has suffered the worst but even then it's only cuts and bruises. He is vaguely aware that something had fallen across him, protecting him from being crushed by the beams and burning timber which had crashed down around him.

"If you'll excuse me I have other patients to—"

"Wait," Stasko says, grabbing him by the arm. "My . . . friend. Do you know if she was brought in also?"

The doctor shakes his head. "I'm sorry, there's a lot of confusion right now. We haven't managed to identify most of those brought in so far but I'm sure if you check back later we'll be able to give you some information."

"I really need to find her."

The doctor sighs. "What is her name?"

"Katja."

"What does she look like?"

"Medium height. Shaved head. Tattoos across her chest."

Stasko's voice turns to a whisper as he describes her, his hand drifting across his own throat, mirroring the way he had earlier stroked her freshly inserted trach tube.

The doctor nods. "I remember her. Bed 13, at least when she was brought in. I think she was okay—"

And before he can finish Stasko is already hobbling away, past a row of gurneys lined up next to one another, empty and blood-stained, past the reception desk. Each bed has a plastic plate mounted onto its head, held in place by cable ties, large black numbers embossed on it.

He finds bed 13 empty.

His heart sinks as he stands next to it, running his fingers across the indentation left behind. And so she is gone again, taken from him. Perhaps Bridget is correct about the girl not being right for the project. Perhaps she isn't the fitting replacement for Anna that he thought she was. Anna, at least, had been willing and although he feels certain that the punk would have come around to the idea of her transformation—at what cost? It had seemed such a perfect moment to have seen Katja's poster that night but now it is beginning to feel fraudulent, that he had been tricking himself in a moment of desperation.

He turns and walks away, trying instead to spot the distinctive pink shock of Bridget's hair, only now thinking of how she might be or even if she is there at all. He starts to cough, his esophagus raw and burning as if he were still breathing in the hot smoke from the fire, holding out a hand to a nearby wall for support.

Someone brushes past him, leaving behind a flowery scent-trail which cuts through the medicinal stench and is instantly recognisable.

"Anna?"

He looks up and sees the scent's source walking away from him, their back to him. Shaven head. Barefoot. A skimpy leopard-print dress.

A vision of utter beauty.

And then she turns her head.

Stasko's world comes to a complete halt.

He *is* wrong about Katja. She *isn't* the one.

His misery had tricked him that night but now his mind is clear.

The creature turns away again and stalks into the corridor beyond the ER.

Stasko, a strange bliss now blooming within him, goes after her.

46.

With the Policie officer chasing after them, Katja and Nikolai charge towards the hospital's radiology suite. They collide with a group of doctors in deep conversation, and then duck around a corner, the officer's shouts echoing past them. They race ahead and then around one corner and then another.

A sign overhead reads *Main Entrance* but Katja grabs Nikolai when he starts towards it, pulling him in the opposite direction. They go through a set of doors, emerging into a dimly lit carpeted room lined with the sort of cheap plastic chairs found at low-rent conference halls. Spread out across three of the chairs which have been neatly aligned, a medical student is fast asleep. They creep around him as the sounds of the Policie officer's boots thud past in the corridor outside, and exit through a door on the opposite side of the room.

"Where are we going?" Nikolai asks.

"We need to find another way out than the main entrance," she tells him once they are out of the room again. "They might be waiting for us there."

"Who might?"

"The trannies, Dimebag Dexter, that fucked-up surgeon . . . take your pick," she answers as they reach another junction. A man in a bright green gown approaches one way so she takes the other.

They travel only a few metres before she stops suddenly.

"Shit."

"What?"

Before she can answer he too recognises that they've hit a dead end. They both turn and are about to go back the way they came when Katja holds up a hand to block Nikolai. She nods at the floor in front of them and at the neat trail of blood that describes their route. She checks herself quickly then looks at Nikolai and her eyes go wide. Another drop of blood escapes his head wound and splashes to the ground.

"Oh," he says.

"If anyone was trying to follow us . . ."

Her words, and the implication, drifts. She grabs his head and for a moment he thinks she is going to beat the shit out of him for being so careless then he feels something being pressed against his wound. The sleeve of her t-shirt. She pushes it against him in an attempt to help it clot then steps back. Tears at the garment, ripping a chunk of it away where the seam has already started to come loose.

"Here," she says, offering him the chunk of fabric. "Now let's get a move on before . . ."

"Before what?" Nikolai asks, pressing the piece of t-shirt to his wound.

But she's looking right past him. Her eyes going wider still.

He follows her gaze and sees Lady D coming towards them.

47.

The debt collector having now seen them and charging towards them, together Katja and Nikolai rush back to the junction. They duck around the corner and into the opposite corridor, the snap of the transvestite's heels ricocheting around the floors and ceiling. They quicken their pace, going round another corner and then another, starting to put distance between them and their pursuer. Katja grabs an empty instrument trolley as they race past it and pulls it into the corridor behind them. A few moments later there's a crashing noise and Katja turns in time to see Lady D tumbling to the ground over the cart.

They hurry onwards until Katja stops and pushes open a door.

"Here!" she shouts, shoving Nikolai inside.

She closes the door behind them, locks it, and they hurry down a short ramp into near-darkness. A wet heat washes over them and there's the smell of fresh laundry. A row of washing machines line one wall, each one rattling and humming, the glow from their displays the only illumination in the room.

"Look for an exit!" she says. "There might be a loading bay or something."

"I can't see anything!" Nikolai replies, clumsily feeling his way along one wall then shrieking when he places a hand on a scalding hot pipe.

"Quiet!" Katja snaps. She palms her way through the darkness, looking for any slivers of light which might indicate a way out but can't find any. "Shit!"

"Katja, where are you?"

"Here." She puts a hand on his shoulder. Then, "There's no other way out. We're going to have to go back up."

48.

"Motherfucker," the woman growls.

Stasko looks at her, sprawled on the floor of the empty corridor next to the fallen cart, one long and beautiful leg spread out to the side, the ankle at the end of it red and slightly swollen. She reaches up to a nearby window ledge with one manicured hand and tries to pull herself upright but slips and she slumps back down again. The passageway's lighting frames her, surrounds her in an angelic glow.

He takes a step towards her, offers a hand. "Here," he says, "let me help."

She instantly snaps around the way a fighting dog might.

"Who the fuck are you?"

For a moment Stasko can't speak, so struck is he by her beauty. Her skull is perfectly shaped and shadowed by stubble. Her eyes are dark yet luminous, her frame strong yet delicate.

"You are *perfection*," he says as he crouches next to her, the words a mere whisper.

"Excuse me?"

"When I saw you in the ER I knew that you were . . . but now, now I see you up close you are even more . . ."

He clasps a hand over his mouth to control his emotions.

"Look, I don't know who the hell you think I am but—"

"You're the one," he interrupts.

"Is that right?" she says, getting to her feet. She winces when she first puts weight on the ankle, easing herself away from him. "Well that may well be the case but I'm afraid I don't have the time right now to—"

She stops when she sees the syringe in his hand.

"Oh for fuck's sake, not again," she says just before he stabs it into her neck.

49.

The day, it seems, is nothing but an infinite see-saw between consciousness and unconsciousness.

This time Lady D comes to with a start. Something is strapped across her chest, preventing her from raising herself any higher than a few inches. The harsh whiteness of the hospital has been swallowed by darkness but the smell of disinfectant and antiseptic hand gel is still strong in the air. A multi-coloured cloud hovers before her, following her gaze as she shifts it from side to side. It pulses in time with the pounding in her head but is quickly fading.

She tries to move her arms and legs but they too are held in place, pain igniting across her ankles and wrists. She hears movement—rustling, smothered breathing – then a bright pinprick of light shines at her. It hits her eyes as if it were a solid shard and she pushes herself back into the bed she is laid out on, twisting her head from side to side to get away from it.

A hand grabs her face, squeezing her cheeks together. It turns her towards the source of the light and she can only just make out a figure behind it wearing a disposable surgical smock and mask. Her thoughts tumble into place and she remembers the man who had helped her to her feet before dosing her with sedative.

"Stay quiet," he says, still gripping her face.

She snaps her head to one side, pulls herself free, then drags phlegm from the back of her throat and spits it at him. "Fuck you."

The man leans over her, the little pen-light he has tilting to more fully illuminate him. His eyes are dark, his pupils fully dilated. He looks her up and down, running a hand up her leg. Lady D jolts her body, doing what she can to resist him whilst still held by the bonds. Another inch or two and he may be in for an unwelcome surprise.

"Now, now," the man whispers to her, his hand skipping to her torso then sweeping across her head. "Don't be afraid, I'm not going to harm you. You don't have to hide yourself from me."

And he holds something up for her to see—the bandage-like wrapping that is the final, outer layer of her gaff.

"No . . ." The word escapes Lady D's lips as a gasp at the suddenly realized exposure.

"It's okay, it's okay," the man says, bundling the fabric up into a little ball. "Transformation is natural. It is vital. I know how you must feel."

"Get me the fuck out of here right now," Lady D says through gritted, and finely polished, teeth. "You have no idea who I am."

The man tilts his head to one side, pulls the mask away from his face and lets it hang beneath his jaw. "I think it's *you* who has no idea who you are," he tells her. "But I can help you with that."

He's gone for a moment or two then returns with another syringe and a plastic bite plate. He places the plate into her mouth, wrapping the elasticated band it is attached to around the back of her head.

"As soon as I've got you out of here and back to my lab, we can begin. . . ."

He removes the syringe's protective cap and gives it a quick tap and squirt to get rid of air bubbles. Lady D struggles once more but the bonds, cable-ties, she realizes, hold firm, biting into her and drawing blood. She refuses to give up, however, twisting and pulling on them, grimacing as the pain builds, grunting and whining behind the bit.

"Hold still," the man says, smacking her inner arm to encourage her veins to swell. "We can't have you thrashing about like this."

The sharp pain of the needle presses against her; her struggle intensifies, her anger and frustration builds as if it will explode from within her.

And then light floods across them.

"Who the hell . . . ?" the man says.

Lady D turns, looks towards the entrance to the room. A woman stands there, her eyes shimmering with tears, her cheeks stained with diluted eye makeup. Lady D blinks rapidly, urging her vision to clear.

"Get out of my way," the man snaps, pulling on the gurney Lady D is strapped to, positioning it between himself and the woman. "Can't you see I have a patient here? She needs to go to surgery *immediately*, do you understand?"

"You're not going anywhere," the woman says, standing firm. "You have no idea who I am do you?"

"I have no *interest* in who you are," the man says, jabbing the gurney towards her as if it were a weapon.

In response the woman takes a gun from her bag. Points it at the surgeon.

And her captor may not recognise the woman but Lady D now does. After all it was only a couple of hours since she had kidnapped her.

50.

Liz peers around the corner of the alleyway she had ducked into after being told by Bridget to leave and get to her safe house. After walking away from the vehicle it had been her every intention to go straight to an old friend who would ask no questions about her need to hide, but with each step she had taken her confidence had waned. She'd eventually turned a corner when she knew that she would be out of Bridget's sight, before cutting through into the alley and doubling back on herself. She'd kept a close eye on Bridget, the smells of Chinese food drifting from a vent above her, until she saw a pair of headlights in the distance and a station wagon pull up alongside her.

Now she watches the figure within the car lean across and talk with Bridget who, moments later, gets out and climbs into his vehicle. When the door opens an internal light comes on and identifies Stasko as the driver. For several moments Liz fights with herself, suddenly certain that something awful is about to happen, that Stasko somehow knows what they are planning. Her fingernails dig into the soft mortar between the wall's bricks.

The internal light goes out and Stasko pulls away. The car comes towards her then fizzes past, spraying up water from the pools on the road, the vehicle's red tail-lights illuminating the shower of droplets. Liz rushes to Bridget's abandoned car and gratefully finds the key tucked under the driver's seat where Bridget often leaves it—right next to a small handgun. Liz takes both, starts the engine, the tail-lights of Stasko's car only just visible in the distance.

She presses down on the accelerator and chases after them.

51.

The doorman is talking to a group of girls as Liz approaches the Wheatsheaf but somehow senses her presence and sticks out an arm to block her way.

"You want in you gotta pay like everyone else," he says, then smiles at the girls to check they are suitably impressed.

Liz checks her bag first but finds no cash there, then checks her pockets. One by one they turn up empty. The doorman's patience is quickly dwindling.

"Look, you want in or—"

"Here," Liz says, holding up a small pile of crumpled notes.

He takes them from her, unfolding them and straightening them one at a time, clearly taking pleasure in elongating the whole process. Liz refuses to show her frustration, knowing that it will only make him delay further. The doorman rolls a piece of bright pink chewing gum around in his mouth before sighing and stepping to one side.

Liz pushes her way through those lingering in the entrance corridor, blaringly loud punk music rampaging off every wall. Stage lights flash and flicker from red to green to blue and back again, sweeping across those gathered there, strobing. The whole place is jumping, people grabbing one another, headbutting anyone close by, as much a battleground as a venue.

Liz makes her way through as the crowd jostles around her, shoving her in several directions but always back into the corridor again. She pushes herself up onto tip-toes and spots the unmistakable burst of pink that is Bridget's hair but can't see any sign of Stasko.

A leering punk looms in front of her, blocking her view. He smiles at her with his sole remaining tooth, his arms held wide as if about to embrace her, chest bare and soaked in beer.

Liz moves to one side but he moves the same way. She ducks to the other side and he follows.

She jumps up and down, looking for Bridget once again and the man copies her, thinking she is pogo-ing and grinning madly now. Over his shoulder she sees the pink hair again and in the same instant someone grabs Bridget.

The man keeps jumping in front of her, blocking her view. And are those flames flickering behind the stage?

"Fuck off!" she shouts, the words lost but the sentiment clear. Something is happening on the stage, the music stopping, just guitar now, but she is only peripherally aware of it.

She jumps again and this time the snapshot is Bridget with a hand around her throat. Liz cries out and charges forwards but the punk catches her, embraces her. She fights to get out of his clutches and then he suddenly lets go. She staggers backwards and the man frowns. He looks up.

Liz follows his gaze just in time to see multiple chunks of debris tumble from the ceiling above and crash into the circle pit. Then the sound of metal rending, of rivets popping, the sounds that echo through the belly of a ship just before the hull bursts and water comes crashing in.

The punk looks at her again, no longer jumping. His face is slack, his eyes wide.

This is just before the ceiling collapses on top of him.

52.

When Liz comes to clouds of dark grey dust swirl around her, carried on the drafts created by the fires that burn everywhere. She's aware of another, cooler breeze brushing over her and thinks that she has somehow ended up outside the club—then realizes that the entire place is now, technically, outside. The remainder of the corridor she had been unable to get out of is steepled over her and several others.

She rolls onto her back and sees that most of the Wheatsheaf is gone, all except a single wall. There are piles of warped scaffold and chunks of masonry out of which various limbs protrude. People cry and moan. Others shout instructions.

Someone runs past her in a green uniform.

Liz pulls herself upright, wincing as pain shoots up her back. Her ears are ringing. Everything is so distant. Another green uniform—a paramedic. A series of ambulances are lined up on the street outside, a cordon being set up by Policie officers just beyond them, holding back a growing crowd. Lights flash red and blue, just as they had during the gig.

Liz becomes aware of a warmth on her left arm and looks down to see blood oozing down it from a gash in her bicep, distorting her tattoos. She picks up her bag, laying beside her, and slings it over her shoulder.

"Bridget . . ." she says, though deaf to her own words thanks to the ringing.

She crawls out of the remains of the corridor through the wreckage on hands and knees, aware of others getting to their feet and stumbling around, some collected by paramedics, others collapsing to the ground once more. She calls out Bridget's name over and over, her arms shaking and threatening to give way but she refuses to stop.

She passes the body of the doorman, his arms spread out beside his head, the night's takings spilling from his bomber jacket pocket, then spots a flash of pink a few metres away. She drags herself over to the prone form, almost hidden beneath the figure of a transvestite in a gold lamé dress.

"Bridget?"

She reaches out and touches the other woman's arm.

She pushes aside the Tgirl's body, rolling it off Bridget. Bridget is covered in a thick layer of concrete dust and charred embers, one leg twisted at an unnatural angle.

"Bridget?"

No response.

She cries out for help and catches the attention of one of the paramedics who quickly finishes tending to another casualty and hurries across. He stops next to Liz, looking down at Bridget next to her. Shakes his head.

Before she can say anything he rushes off again, then there is the sound of one of the ambulance's sirens blaring into life and the screech of its tyres. Liz cries out to him but he either doesn't hear her or doesn't care.

"Please . . ." Liz begs. She reaches out to Bridget's still form, this time noticing how cold the other woman is when she makes contact. She looks around, desperate for someone else to help her despite knowing that it's all too late, calling to anyone who will listen to help her. She lifts Bridget's hand and peels one of the purple gloves off, the latex already torn in places. She strokes the soft skin of Bridget's palm, pressing it to her face.

Then looks up—and spots Stasko. He is being lifted onto a gurney by a pair of paramedics who then strap him into place and wheel him towards another waiting ambulance.

A vicious fury ignites inside Liz.

She places Bridget's hand back down and forces herself to her feet, her knees threatening to give way at first, then stabilising. A gust of hot air washes over her from a nearby fire, the image of Stasko being loaded into the ambulance shimmering and diluting in the heat distortion.

Liz bears down on the pain and staggers towards the vehicle but isn't even close when its siren comes to life and it speeds away from the scene. She keeps going regardless, holding out one arm towards it, as if she could simply pluck it from the road, until someone catches her wrist.

A young paramedic, smeared in blood and dark, grimy dust.

"Miss, you can't . . . please . . . are you okay? Are you hurt?"

She stares past him at the ambulance vanishing into the distance.

"Where are they going?" she asks him. "Where are they taking him?"

"St. Michael's," he tells her, noticing the wound on her shoulder. "Let me get someone to look at that for you—"

She pushes him away, clutching her bag close to her, but he won't let her go. He calls to another paramedic loading up an ambulance, asks if they have room for one more. There's a short argument which Liz is only vaguely aware of, still staring at the point where Stasko's ambulance was last visible. She breaks free, ignoring the pleas of the paramedic and making her way towards, then through, the cordon. The Policie who guard it see her coming and let her through, watching her stagger off across the street.

Her mind somehow spinning and numb simultaneously, she continues on across the junction to the corner where she had left Bridget's car. Gets in and takes the key from her bag and starts the engine.

An ambulance reverses away from the smouldering remains of the Wheatsheaf and into the junction then the wheels spin as it changes direction and plows forwards. Liz throws the car into first, ignoring the old gearbox's resistance, and goes after it.

53.

She abandons the car in the hospital's parking lot, the drop-off points at the building's entrance jam-packed with ambulances hurriedly unloading their bloodied cargo. She puts the gun into her bag then walks inside, vibrating with adrenaline, knowing that if she were to give in to her body's demands and slump into a heap then the pain which lurks at the edges of her consciousness will flood in and consume her.

So she keeps going, following the main flow of traffic into the ER, feeling as if she exists on a different plane of reality than everyone around her. She approaches the circular reception desk, stepping around and between the frenzied medical staff. A large whiteboard hangs above it, names and numbers scribbled on it.

She scans it until she finds Stasko's name, grateful that he had been carrying some form of ID, then takes note of the bed number. She goes to the nearest bed, reads its number, then tracks her way towards where Stasko would be. She stops, and sees the man being helped from the bed by a medic. They have a brief conversation then Stasko walks across the ER, obviously looking for something specific. He stops at bed thirteen, finds it vacant, then turns around. For a moment he appears to be lost then his expression changes. He's staring at something across the busy emergency room but Liz can't quite tell what. Then he's moving again.

Liz hurries after him, keeping her distance. She chases him deeper into the hospital, always making sure to remain a corner or junction behind him, then hears a crashing sound up ahead. She slows, grateful that they are now well away from the busy emergency room and in the quieter passageways of unused examination rooms and locked offices.

She can hear him up ahead, carefully peeks around the corner. He's helping a woman to her feet, then says something to her. Liz watches as he withdraws a syringe from one of his pockets and flicks the cap away. Plunges it into the woman's neck. Then she continues to watch as he slips an arm under the woman's and hauls her to her feet then drags her into one of the nearby rooms.

It's only then that Liz recognises who it is that Stasko is taking away and realizes that it is not a woman after all—instead the man who had abducted her earlier, the one Bridget had tricked.

So Stasko *was* involved in . . . whatever that had been.

She edges towards the room, listens at the door. From inside there is shuffling, then a ripping sound. Drawers being opened and closed.

Liz has no idea what she is witnessing but also no longer cares.

She waits for a few minutes to see if Stasko will emerge but her patience withers quickly. She checks that nobody is around and opens her bag. The gun glints within.

She opens the door.

Stasko spins around. The captor, cable-tied to a gurney beside him.

"Get out of my way," he snaps. "Can't you see I have a patient here? She needs to go to surgery *immediately*, do you understand?"

"You're not going anywhere," Liz tells him. "You have no idea who I am do you?"

Tears are welling up within her now, her hatred of him filling her with a dark, menacing energy. The thought of Bridget lying on the ground outside the club that the surgeon had dragged her to, her internal organs ground to a pulp, fills her mind.

"I have no *interest* in who you are," Stasko says, jabbing the gurney at her.

Liz reaches in and takes out the gun. Her hand shakes uncontrollably as she raises it to point it at him. She clenches her teeth, focusing all of her hatred into her arm, then her hand, then her forefinger.

And once that happens, it's like the trigger pulls itself.

54.

"Here, here," Nikolai says.

Katja follows his voice to the back of the room, fumbling through the darkness. She collides with a laundry basket, pushes it to one side.

"Laundry chute," he says. There's the sound of metal grinding against metal as she heaves the hatch before him upwards.

Katja reaches past him. "It's too small," she says, slapping her hands against the sheers walls of the chute. "And there's no way we could climb up it anyway."

"What about down? It must lead down to a main laundry room – that'll surely have a way out, a collection point."

"It's too small, Nik, up or down."

"So what about a trolley? I'll find some used scrubs, you could climb inside and I'll wheel you out."

"What do you think this is, a fucking cartoon? I'm *not* getting into one of those beside bloody clothes and shitty underwear. Anyway she's just as likely to spot you as she is me. There's no other option, we're going to have to go back up."

"And if she's waiting there for us?"

"If she'd seen us come in here she would have bust in already."

"Maybe not."

"We don't have any other choice, Nik!"

And without waiting for him she feels her way along the wall back to the ramp and starts to climb it. A moment later Nikolai follows. They stop at the door and she listens through it but there's nothing to hear.

"Ready?" she whispers.

Nikolai shrugs and she shoves the door open before he can say or do anything else.

The corridor is empty, the strip-lighting above reflected like a meandering river on the recently polished floor.

Katja looks back the way they came and sees the toppled cart that the debt collector had crashed into, but no sign of the woman herself. Perhaps they have gotten away from her after all.

"Which way?"

"Not that way," Katja says, nodding towards the fallen cart. "This way."

She jogs farther up the corridor, ducks around a corner to a pair of lifts, Nikolai following.

"If we can get to where that chute leads there should be a way out."

She hits both of the buttons, illuminating them, then takes a step back to watch the level indicators above each set of doors. One remains where it is but the other is already ticking through the numbers.

Five.

Four.

She isn't sure if it was already moving before she pressed it, if someone else was on their way down.

Three.

Suddenly thinks that Nikolai's idea to dress themselves in smocks might not have been that bad after all but knows it's too late now.

Two.

The elevator dings and then the doors slide open to reveal not Lady D but a male nurse. He stands in the middle of the elevator, staring down at his feet, mumbling something to himself.

He looks up when the doors open and his eyes go wide.

Nobody says anything. Nobody moves.

"Are you getting out or what?" Katja asks.

The man opens his mouth to say something, glances at Nikolai, then grabs Katja and pulls her into the elevator. Whilst Nikolai's brain is still processing what is going on the nurse jabs at the buttons inside the elevator and the doors slide shut.

And Katja is gone.

55.

Lady D twists away from the woman brandishing the gun just before it fires. The bullet flies over Lady D's head, her already-damaged hearing suffering another blow from the sound of the shot.

Stasko is thrown backwards by the force of the gunshot, spinning him around and into the gurney to which Lady D is still tied. His head smacks off the rail and he slumps to the ground and out of her sight. The woman stands in the doorway, tears rolling down her cheeks, the weapon still in her shaking hands.

Lady D doesn't take her eyes off the woman but with her left hand she quietly feels around the instrument trolley which has been knocked adjacent to her after Stasko had swung the gurney between himself and his attacker. Her fingers brush across something cold and wafer-thin—a blade.

The other woman takes a step forward, blinking away tears, knuckles whitened from her grip on the gun. Stasko's breathing is wet and laboured.

"You took her from me," she says, her upper lip curling like a dog about to bite. "You always took her from me."

The woman's attention fully on Stasko, Lady D moves the blade between her fingers, manoeuvring it until she can work it back and forth across the cable tie. She has to twist her wrist at an almost impossible angle, the tendons there burning, working blind, not wanting to risk the woman seeing what she is doing, until finally the cable-tie snaps and her arm comes free.

The woman kneels down beside Stasko, out of Lady D's sight. Lady D quickly cuts through the tie around her other wrist then does the same with those around her ankles. She peers over the edge of the bed. Stasko grips his chest, wet with blood. It trickles out from between his fingers and the corners of his mouth.

The woman's finger twitches on the trigger but she's gotten too close to her prey and before she can pull it Stasko snatches the gun from her. He momentarily struggles with the weapon, his hands wet with blood, turning it to point at the woman. She tries to grab it back from him but this time there is no delay, no hesitation. No words.

Just action.

He pulls the trigger and the woman falls backwards, crashing into the door.

Lady D jumps at the sound but stays where she is, biding her time, waiting for the right moment.

Stasko hauls himself to his feet, reaching out for support from the gurney, leaving a smeared trail of red along it. His breathing even more wet and laboured as he levels the gun at the woman's head.

"I still don't care who you are," he says.

And that's when Lady D lashes out.

She swings a leg around, her foot slamming into his shooting arm and the weapon flies through the air, closely followed by her high heel. Stasko cries out and she leaps from the bed, rushing towards the gun before he can recover it. She punches him in the back of the head as he scrambles towards the weapon, flooring him instantly. She picks up the gun in one hand, the heel in the other. Slots the gun into a belt that draws her waist in to unreasonable dimensions and wields the heel like a hammer.

Stasko gets up, the blood dripping from his gunshot wound joined by that dripping from his split lip. Lady D grabs his hair and jerks his head up so that he's looking her in the eyes.

"*I* decide what I want to be," she says. "*Not* you."

And then she smashes the shoe into the side of his head, aiming for his temple but connecting somewhere just beyond it. He cries out and threatens to topple but she keeps a firm grip on his hair and delivers another blow; another; another.

She lets him drop to the ground but keeps hitting him, all the rage and tension which have built up over the course of the day finally finding an outlet, and she doesn't stop until she is utterly exhausted and Stasko is no longer breathing. Her arm is locked up, her fingers clawed around the shoe. Stasko's face is nothing but splattered pulp.

"There's your fucking transformation," she says, wiping blood from her face and chest.

She turns to the woman, slumped against the door, a neat dark hole drilled into the very centre of her chest. It doesn't look good.

"Liz? It's Liz, right?" Lady D asks, snapping the woman into focus.

Liz nods vaguely.

"I'll go get you some help," Lady D says but Liz reaches out to stop her.

"I did what I came to do," she says.

Lady D notices the scorch marks on the woman's t-shirt, the oily grime that smears her tattoos.

"You were at the Wheatsheaf? What about Soelberg? If I can find her I . . ."

Liz shakes her head, spilling more tears, and Lady D knows from the look in the woman's eyes what it means.

"I'm sorry," Lady D says. "If I'd have known things were going to . . ."

She fumbles with the sentiment until it deserts her completely.

Instead she takes Liz's hand in her own, so covered in Stasko's blood that it is as if she is wearing a glove. The woman squeezes on it and when she smiles at Lady D, the debt collector is certain that Liz is seeing something else. Someone else.

Then Liz's eyes roll back into her skull and her hand slides away.

Lady D remains there for a few moments, reluctant to leave the woman, then gets up. She examines the shoe she had beaten Stasko with and it is as covered in the surgeon's blood as her hand. No point in even attempting to wipe it down. When she slips it on it's like putting her foot into someone's body cavity.

At least it's warm.

She steps out into the corridor, thankful that it remains deserted. Spots the cart she had collided with a little farther up and so quickly gathers her bearings. The attack on Stasko has relieved some of her tension and replaced it with a new vigour, a new determination to end this whole night once and for all.

All she wants is her money, plain and simple.

And nothing, nobody, will stop her from getting it.

56.

Nikolai stares at his reflection in the old metal of the elevator, the confused look on his face echoed back in a warped version of itself. Above him the elevator light slides from left to right as it climbs the floors again, taking Katja with it. He slaps at the buttons but the elevator ignores him and continues to climb.

And then he sees the distorted shape of a figure behind him. He spins around.

Looking like something out of the final scene of a Takashi Miike film, Lady D walks towards him. Blood splatters the dress she wears and one of her heels is crooked and similarly soaked in gore. Her wig is partially flattened on one side and unravelling at the back.

There's a gun tucked into her belt but apparently she doesn't feel the need to draw it.

"Where is she? Where's the punk?"

"I . . . uh . . . we . . ."

"Where's my *money*?" Lady D growls, taking another step closer.

Nikolai backs up against the elevator door. "I don't . . . she split. I don't know where . . ."

Lady D is now close enough that she blocks out the light and so becomes nothing more than a silhouette before Nikolai. She leans forwards, one arm planted on the wall beside him. Looks up at the floor numbers being lit one by one then back to Nikolai.

Now the gun comes out.

"Do I look like I'm in the mood to be fucked with?"

"Not really."

Lady D plants her other arm on the other side of Nikolai, pinning him in place.

"*So where is she?*"

"Someone took her," Nikolai says, pointing up at the numbers above. "The doors opened and someone just . . . took her."

Nose to nose now. The debt collector's spicy perfume is mixed with the scent of burnt metal and antiseptic.

"What did I just say?" she warns him.

"I'm telling you, someone grabbed her. A nurse—or someone dressed like one."

"They were already in there waiting for her?"

Nikolai nods. "But he looked . . . surprised."

"He knew who she was?"

"I don't know . . . I suppose so. He appeared to recognise her. I think so anyway."

Lady D lets out a long, deep sigh and straightens up, stands back from him.

"Is there *anyone* who isn't after this little bitch?"

Nikolai doesn't know whether she's expecting an answer or not. She's looking up at the illuminated floor numbers again. The elevators illuminated numbers have settled on the floor above them.

She hits the button to call the elevators back but they remain where they are.

"Fine," she says. "We'll take the stairs."

"We?" Nikolai asks just before she grabs his arm.

"We," she confirms, and pushes him ahead of her, the gun nudging his back. "And whoever it is that took her—they're going to give her back."

57.

Katja feels the swelling on her face before she has even fully come to, focused around three sharp spikes of pain where the guitar strings had punctured her flesh.

She tries to move but can't. Of course.

The room she is in is dimly lit but retains a medicinal tang which makes it clear she is still in the hospital. This is confirmed when she looks around as much as her restraints will allow. The main overhead lights are off, just the little wall-mounted ones are on, their glow soft and orangey. The privacy curtain is half-drawn around her bed.

She hears footsteps and the man who grabbed her and smacked her over the head with her own guitar appears beside her. He still wears a nurses uniform but the first few buttons are undone, revealing varied necklaces of wooden beads beneath. He watches her anxiously, rubbing the beads, avoiding eye contact.

"What do you want?" she asks him.

He rubs the beads harder, looks past her, through the curtain.

"What he wants doesn't matter," a voice says from the other side of the plastic sheet. "What *I* want, however, does."

And despite the distortion which layers it—she knows that voice.

The nurse takes the curtain in one hand and walks around her, pulling it with him as he goes. It reveals another bed parallel to Katja's own, next to a large broad window which runs along one wall, blinds half-shuttered across it. The bed is empty but someone is sitting next to it, strapped into a contraption that is part wheelchair, part portable life-support unit. His legs and arms are strapped into place, a belt across his chest, IV lines warping around him like refracted light, the neck brace which tips his chin upwards exposing a line of thick scar tissue.

And when she realizes who it is, she wonders if perhaps the blow to the head was heftier than she had first thought because it can't be, it just can't be.

But it is.

It is.

58.

A middle-aged man appears at the top of the stairs and his jaw drops when he sees the two coming towards him. Nikolai stops moving, the barrel of the gun pressing deep into the soft muscle of his back and he grunts in pain.

Lady D looks past him at the man, whose mouth opens a little farther in response to the sight of the blood-soaked debt collector.

"What?" she says, challenging him.

The man makes an abrupt U-turn and is gone, the sound of his hurried steps squeaking off the vinyl flooring and into the distance. Lady D gives Nikolai another shove to get him going again until they reach the second floor.

There's a set of locked double-doors and a sign on the wall beside them details the strict visiting conditions of the High Dependency Unit along with instructions to press the buzzer for attention. A small security camera is embedded in the wall just above the door entry system.

Lady D swears under her breath.

Hits the buzzer.

A few moments pass then there's a crackle of static and a voice says "Sorry, visiting hours are over."

Lady D positions herself before the camera in such a way as to ensure they won't get a clear view of her. "It's security," she says.

"Security? What's wrong?"

"We believe an unauthorised person may have gotten into your ward. They were being pursued by my colleagues and they came up to this floor. Please open the door."

"Nobody's come in here, only—"

"Miss, please, this is urgent. The lives of your patients may be in danger."

A pause. "Hold on," she says.

"Fuck this up and I'll kill you, understand?" Lady D tells Nikolai as she stands back and readies herself.

He nods then the door opens, just a little at first. A nurse peers through cautiously.

Lady D immediately shoves the door open, sending the woman flying backwards but she quickly gathers herself and then she's running back to the nurse's station a few metres away. The debt collector gives chase as best she can in her fractured heels.

The nurse throws herself at the desk, knocking aside the cheap erotica novel she had been reading, and reaches for a phone just a few inches away but Lady D snatches the woman's arm and pulls her away, throws her to the ground.

"No you don't," Lady D says, then strikes the woman across the head with her gun. She hits the ground then just lies there, utterly still.

The debt collector's eyes narrow and she circles around the desk. "Shit."

"What is it?" Nikolai asks.

"Panic alarm," she says. "Bitch was going for that, not the phone. Which means they're probably already on their way."

She grabs the swivel chair from behind the desk, hurries back to the double doors and wedges it beneath the horizontal metal handle which opens them. Grabs another couple of plastic ones set aside for visitors and grieving relatives and stacks them all against one another, entangling their legs, wedging them together. Then she smashes at the door entry system, popping the plastic cover away to reveal the electronics beneath then smashing them further with the grip of the gun.

"Won't hold them for long," she mutters, aiming the gun at Nikolai once more.

Nikolai glances at the heating pipes running down the wall beside them and briefly visualises himself shoving Lady D's gun hand into one of them, searing her flesh and knocking the weapon from her grasp then making a run for it.

Then bullets slamming into his back and head and him crumpling to the ground, a bloody mess.

"Whoever took her could have gotten her out of the hospital but they didn't," Lady D says. "They brought her up here instead."

"To a high dependency unit? What for?"

"Whatever it is, they must have a good reason. We're going to check each and every room until we find her, do you understand me?"

Nikolai nods, his compliance encouraged by the pistol barrel currently bruising his spine. Beyond the alcove the corridor is quiet, each door closed, the lights turned down low. The sense of misery is as pervasive as the hum of life support machines vibrating through the floor and walls.

Nikolai hovers as Lady D approaches the first door. When she notices he isn't following her she curls a lip and gestures silently with the gun.

Nikolai shakes his head, refusing.

Anger briefly flares in her at his resistance until she notices that he is now the same pallor as the grimy flooring. His eyes are wide, fixated on a whiteboard on the wall beside her.

"Uh oh."

"What? What is it?"

Lady D scans the board, looking for whatever it is that is concerning him more than the threat of being shot.

He says nothing but his hands are shaking.

"Nikolai!" she snaps in a whisper, hearing the squeak of rubber shoes somewhere nearby.

He points at the board the way a victim might identify their attacker in a line-up, still petrified despite the safety glass between them. "That name," he says. "I know that name."

"What name?" Lady D asks, scanning the list of patients and their room numbers.

Nikolai takes a step closer to the board, pressing his finger into it hard enough to smear the name he is identifying. "That one," he says, then turns to her.

"Kohl," he says. "Vladimir Kohl."

59.

A bead of sweat rolls down Kohl's brow, kinking at an indentation in his forehead and sweeping down to his eyebrow. He blinks it away but it seeps into the hairs before emerging at the top of his eyelid then trickling into his eye.

His hands are lifeless, strapped to the chair in which he is seated not to prevent him from moving them but to prevent them from slipping off without him being able to reposition them again. If they dropped they would just sit there, blood gathering within them and perhaps building up a little clot that would soon work its way up into his brain and end the torture of blinding drips of his own sweat and the sounds of fucking coming from through the wall.

Previously he would have welcomed that little bullet of his own plasma, or have just wished he had never been rescued from the boat in the first place—but that was before he had seen the poster.

The door opens and Moonbeam is back, his skin glistening with sweat, his chin stained with lipstick, tucking his shirt back into the standard-issue white trousers. He does up his buttons, once again hiding the beads he wears, and slicks back his hair. Closes the door and smiles at Kohl.

"Mr Kohl," he says, still catching his breath. From the corridor outside, the sounds of footsteps and a curvy figure brushes past the window. "How are we these evening?"

"I'm stuck in a chair unable to move anything other than my index finger and I have to stare at your ugly fucking face every day."

The nurse either doesn't hear Kohl or chooses to ignore him, busying himself with the chart clipped to the end of the patient's bed. He scans it, then clips it back into place, before crossing to Kohl. Kohl can smell the woman on him—her perfume, her body. He closes his eyes for a few moments while Moonbeam checks over the readouts on the bank of little monitors attached to the equipment keeping Kohl alive.

"Your blood pressure is a little high," the nurse says absently. He adjusts a couple of dials on the machines then retrieves a little plastic cup of pills from a nearby trolley. "Open up."

Kohl does so then suddenly snaps his mouth shut. "Red *first*," he says.

Moonbeam looks down at the pill he has tipped into his hand. "They all have to be taken Mr Kohl, you don't have to worry about—"

"Red!" Kohl says, louder this time. "Red then purple then blue then white then yellow-blue split. You of all people should understand the importance of order. Idiot."

The nurse does as instructed, Kohl exuding threat and menace despite his condition, dropping the pills onto the other man's tongue one by one and letting him swallow them.

"All done," Moonbeam says, smiling like a born-again Christian, like a children's TV presenter. "Now I have to go complete my rounds but if there's anything else at all I can get you all you need to do is—"

"I want you to help me kill someone," Kohl says.

The nurse, already starting to walk away, stops in his tracks. "Excuse me?"

"You heard me. My voice still works fine."

Moonbeam laughs nervously, not coming any closer. "I thought you said you wanted me to help you kill—"

"I did," Kohl cuts him off. "Come here."

Moonbeam looks around, perhaps hoping that Kohl was talking to someone else. Anyone else.

"I—"

"Come. Here." Kohl's machines beep and whine as if urging the nurse onwards.

Moonbeam does as instructed, one hand subconsciously going to the beads hidden beneath his uniform. He lingers before Kohl, knowing that the man is utterly chair-bound but still half-expecting him to launch himself at Moonbeam.

"Look out the window, across the street."

"There's no one there."

"On the wall, you moron. The poster."

"Which one?"

"Left-hand side, just above the anarchist stencil," Kohl tells him, the spot memorised after having stared at it for almost the entire evening.

"The . . . punk band?" He squints, trying to make out the writing emblazoned across it but can't manage it.

"She's the one who did this to me. She's obviously tried to change her appearance but I'll never forget that face."

"Mr Kohl, I don't think you quite realize what you're saying."

"Don't patronise me. You're the one always going on about Karma. This is Karma."

"That's not how it works," the nurse says, now fingering one of his necklaces having popped open a button.

"Yeah? Who decides that? God?"

"I don't believe in a deity, the Universe—"

"*Regardless*, here I am, stuck in a chair and left to stare out this fucking window all day and *her* face is plastered up right outside it. You don't think the Universe is trying to tell me something? I'm being given a chance to make things right."

"It's not telling you to *kill* someone, whatever you think they might have done to you."

"But it's telling you to fuck that pretty little thing in the closet next door every night is it? That is, assuming it's not your wife in there with you."

Moonbeam follows Kohl's gaze to the wedding ring on his fingers and he snaps the other hand across it protectively. "I don't know what you're talking about."

"I may be a cripple but I'm not deaf," Kohl says quietly. "And I'm not stupid."

Sensing the nurse's defences weakening, Kohl switches tact. "Then why don't we let the Universe decide what should happen?"

"What do you mean?"

"If we were to, say, just . . . set things in motion. If we did something . . . small . . . then leave Karma to decide what consequences should follow? I mean, we couldn't change what was destined to happen, could we? That's for the Universe to decide."

"Well, yes, that's true but . . ."

"Good. Then all I'm asking is for you to make a few adjustments to the poster."

"What kind of adjustments?"

"So you'll do it?"

"I didn't say that."

"After what she did I won't be the only one after her—others will recognise her too. I may not be able to do much from this chair but they could."

"Killing is a dark energy which the Universe—"

"We're not killing anyone, I already told you that," Kohl insists, keeping his voice level, realising that the softer approach is working more effectively. "At worst it's . . . vandalism. The poster already says where she'll be and when, if someone else out there recognises her and decides to do something . . . well that's their choice isn't it? We're not forcing them. We're barely doing anything at all, really."

The nurse is working his beads again. He keeps glancing out at the poster. He nods his head in reluctant agreement.

"You have a video camera?" Kohl asks.

"What for?"

"I need you to be there—at the gig."

Before the nurse can protest Kohl cuts him off.

"I want to see it when it happens. *If* it happens," he

quickly corrects himself. "I want to see what Karma decides for her. Or," and the change in the tone of his voice makes up for what he can no longer communicate through posture, "I could just tell your superiors about what you've been getting up to and then we could see what Karma decides for *you*."

60.

Ten minutes later Kohl watches through the same window which has been his only view of the world for the past few months as the nurse appears on the street below. The man takes something from inside the dark jacket which covers his uniform and scribbles on the poster.

When he's done he steps back and glances up at Kohl, not able to see the patient in the dark-reflected glass, but knowing he is there. Kohl's mouth twists itself as close as it can to a smile at the sight of the Mohawk and trach tube scrawled onto the image of Katja.

Then the nurse pulls his jacket around himself and walks off, ready to repeat this vandalism across the city.

61.

"Yeah, fuck you, too," the woman growls into the mike and the sound check finishes.

Moonbeam looks around, wondering if any potential attackers would now put in the appearance he had been waiting for throughout the ear-splitting cacophony that had been going on for the last twenty minutes, but the place is even emptier than it had been to start with. It is still likely if anyone had seen the posters then they would wait until the gig proper later that night but he also knows that he can't risk Kohl's wrath by missing anything so he ambles towards the stage, watching as the band slips into the passageway beyond. A heavy in a bomber jacket ensures he can't follow them and so instead he leaves the place and heads around the back—in time to see Katja being confronted by a trio of transvestites.

This is it, he thinks. *Shit, this is it.*

Lingering at the entrance to the back-alley he slips out the video camera he had brought, flinching at the electronic beep which sounds when it is switched on.

He holds the camera up, not sure if he actually wants anything to happen or not, keeps it steadied on them, waiting, just waiting—and then Katja just walks away. He steps back into the shadow of a doorway for safety and watches her leave the alley and make her way up the main street, expecting that the Tgirls would perhaps come chasing after her. But nothing happens.

Kohl will not be happy.

And then he spots the car.

A crapped-out station wagon, it drifts onto the road at a slow speed, keeping its distance from the fast-walking punk up ahead but clearly tracking her, its headlights turned off. Moonbeam hurries to his own vehicle, parked a short distance away, leaving the headlights off and following the flickering brake-lights of the car as it turns again and again to trace Katja's strangely erratic route until suddenly the headlights come on and the car lunges at her. She starts to run but someone leaps from the vehicle. Moonbeam parks and hurriedly fumbles with the camera to get it into position just in time to see the hefty figure crash down on top of her. He films the brief struggle, his stomach churning at the thought that he could be capturing on film a person's final moments, keeps rolling as the man holds a rag to her face then picks up the punk's limp body and dumps her into the rear seat of his car.

Moonbeam zooms in, the camera's crappy lens struggling in the low light, the image grainy and jerky.

Then suddenly there is someone else in the shot, a woman with bright pink hair tied back in a ponytail, wearing gloves of some sort. She stabs something into the neck of the fat man who had grabbed Katja and now he goes limp too. She shoves her hand into the man's overcoat and pulls out his wallet, and for a moment Moonbeam thinks that this is nothing more than a simple mugging as she goes through its contents. But then she drops it and crosses to the car.

Keep filming, Moonbeam tells himself. *Just keep filming, this isn't your fault, whatever happens is Fate, it would have happened anyway.*

The pink-haired woman pulls Katja from the Oldsmobile and checks her pulse before transferring the punk to her own vehicle, parked up a few metres ahead. She pulls away cautiously, slowly, as if not wanting to raise any suspicions.

Moonbeam puts his car back into gear and drifts forwards, headlights still off. He stops the car by the body of the fat man, careful to keep his distance from Miss Pink. The needle sticks out of his neck glinting in the streetlights, the contents of his wallet are scattered around him. Reluctant to leave the safety of his vehicle he opens the door just enough to reach down and picks up a business card.

Detective Dixon DeBoer.

It just keeps getting better.

The fat man, the detective, had taken Katja down viciously, dosed her with something to knock her out. No cuffs, no calling it in. Decidedly unofficial. But Miss Pink had been different, almost caring—some sort of personal protection perhaps?

Moonbeam reaches under his collar for his beads and rubs them rapidly. Miss Pink's rear lights are now far up ahead, almost out of sight.

Kohl would be satisfied with the footage though, wouldn't he? That would be enough, wouldn't it?

Knowing the answer he jumps back in his car, revs the engine and hurries after her.

62.

To a club heavy with the scent of latex and sweat, the furniture all cut-glass edged with black as if a glitzy high rise had been scavenged piece by piece and then re-assembled beneath the blinking neon lights. A semi-circular bar emerges from one wall, polished glasses suspended on wires that run above the bar staff. Red leather sofas, as dark as clotted blood, are arranged in a grid-like pattern, the one nearest him populated by women in a rubber skirts and a man with a shaven, tattooed head. They look up as he enters, clocking his waterproof jacket, the collar of his uniform sticking out slightly, but either don't care that he looks so out of place or are too wasted to notice.

He does his best to look casual as he drifts through the club, following Miss Pink as she hauls Katja's body towards a door at the back, one of the punk's arms wrapped around her shoulder as if merely assisting a drunken friend. She enters a code into a keypad by the door then she's gone. He edges closer, one hand wrapped around the camera hidden inside his jacket, until someone shouts "Can't go back there."

Moonbeam tells them sorry, makes up an excuse about looking for the bathroom, then backs away before they can direct him. Not sure what else to do he sits down on one of the sofas as far away from the smiling transvestite at the other end as he can. He keeps a close watch on the door, every now and again a couple (always a couple but sometimes of the same sex, some times of the opposite) punches in the code and disappears into whatever lies beyond until, eventually, Miss Pink re-emerges—without Katja.

And that is either really good—or really bad.

He grabs an empty glass and pretends to drink from it until the woman has passed and again he thinks, *Is that enough?* He thinks, *Will Kohl be happy now?* He could just leave now and that would be it, the deal done, right?

He grabs his beads and works them, ignoring the Tgirl who scooched herself towards him a few inches without him realising, then gets up suddenly and hurries to a quiet spot at the back. He takes out his phone and dials Kohl's number.

"So?" Kohl answers immediately. His voice is faint through the voice-activated headset Moonbeam had smuggled in and, with difficulty, affixed to Kohl's ear amidst the tubes that encircle the man's head.

"It's uh . . . she's uh . . ."

"Speak up, you idiot, I can barely hear you. Are you still at the gig?"

"No . . . uh . . . I followed her. Someone took her. They have her now."

There is a brief exhalation from Kohl and Moonbeam pictures a smile spreading across the man's face. "Who?"

"First a guy but then this other chick came along, she injected him with something and . . . and then took Katja."

"Took her where?"

"A club. Called uh . . . Flesh Heel I think. I'm there now."

"So where's Katja? What's the woman doing with her?"

"I don't know, she took her through a door in the back then came back out without her."

"Well what are they doing with her?"

"I don't know! Look, man, I'm, going to get out of here, this place has a fucking dark aura and there's a tranny that keeps—"

"You're staying fucking put until you know whether that bitch is getting her due or not. Have you got the camera?"

"Yeah but man, there's something else going on—that other guy, the one that jumped her first? He's a cop, man. A frickin' detective!"

"What makes you think that?"

"Because I'm looking at his frickin' business card right now, man! Detective Dixon DeBoer it says right here!"

"*Dixon DeBoer*? That's who was after her?"

"Yeah. You know him?"

"I know of him. Used to work shipments from the island, made sure no overly keen customs guys got in the way and dealt with them if they did. Took pleasure in it too, from what I heard. Guy's as crooked and nasty as they come."

"Yeah, well, he needs to learn to watch his back 'cause Miss Pink has Katja now and so we're done, right? I did as you asked."

"You're going nowhere you dirty little hippy," Kohl snaps. "DeBoer, I know, would deal with the little bitch but this other one? Find out where she was taken and what they have planned for her and don't you dare think about leaving until you know, you got me? Otherwise the next call I'll be making is to the ward sister—or your wife."

63.

So Moonbeam waits, mixing himself into the crowd, feeling like an antelope singled out by a pride of lionesses, watching as more of the clientele punch in the code, memorising the digits—but there's too many people in his way and he can't risk entering the wrong code. Eventually he moves as close as he dares to the door, pretending to drink from a beer bottle which someone has left behind while making sure that his lips don't make contact with the possibly germ-addled rim. More couples come and go. Those who enter do so with stoned smiles and lustful eyes and those who emerge do so beaded in sweat turned multi-coloured by the club's lights.

Then the rubber-skirted woman he'd seen earlier approaches with a tall, skinny man, leading the man by the hand. Her co-ordination made shaky by the cocktail of drugs she has no doubt filled herself with, she has to type in the code slowly enough that Moonbeam can identify it.

He waits for a few moments after they have gone

inside then approaches the door. He looks around to check nobody is suspicious then punches in the code, hoping that he has identified it correctly. A green light illuminates on the bottom of the pad and there's an audible click. He doesn't want to go through that door, doesn't want to hear it locking behind him and sealing him in with whatever lies beyond. But it is too late to back out now.

Before he can change his mind he pushes the door open, keeping it casual, to look as if this is something he does every night.

And panic floods through him as he almost bumps into Katja.

64.

The mist of body heat swirls around him for a few moments then dissipates in the relative coolness of the short white corridor beyond. The punk stands before him with another man, junky-looking.

"Excuse me," Moonbeam says, making an instant decision on what to do and stepping to one side.

For a moment he is certain that they know exactly who he is and why he is there, then they both push past him and into the club. Moonbeam lets the door click shut again behind him, too busy watching the two figures move through the crowds.

Then hurries after them.

65.

He punches in Kohl's number and once more it's answered before the end of the first ring.

"Well?"

"Well . . ."

"You still at the club? Then where? Did you find her? What did they do to her?" Kohl asks, his voice dripping with glee at the thought of what horrors Katja might have been subjected to.

"She got away," Moonbeam says. "Her and this other . . . someone else. I don't know what the frick was going on there but that is one seriously fricked-up place—"

"Got away?" Kohl says, the words heavy and menacing like a bloodied meat cleaver. "What do you mean she got away?"

"Or they let her go, I don't know. But she left. With a guy. Don't worry, I followed her. They're holed up in some old squat under the Falqué flyover and I'm sitting outside it now."

Kohl mutters something that Moonbeam is glad to not quite catch.

"I give this bitch to them on a plate and everybody's just dicking around. Have you still got DeBoer's number?"

"The cop?"

"Call him. Tell him where she is before they move on. He'll deal with her, I can guarantee it."

"Look, man, why don't you call him you know him so well, you know? I've done what you asked, now . . ."

"First of all I don't know him, I know *of* him—and secondly, *you moron*, I'm in as much shit as Katja after what happened on the island. Why would I be relying on a weasily little piece of muck like you to do all this if I could just call up a contact or two and get them to fuck her over for me?"

"Wait," Moonbeam says but Kohl isn't interested, launching into another bile-and-threat soaked rant but Moonbeam keeps saying it over and over. "Wait. Wait. Just wait a minute! I see her."

"Katja? You see Katja?"

Moonbeam doesn't answer right away and Kohl goes silent, the only thing audible the click and hum of the medical devices he is attached to.

"Miss Pink," Moonbeam says finally, watching the woman emerge from the car parked up ahead. "I'll call you back."

He hangs up, sits upright, leaning towards the dashboard. Picks up the video camera and switches it on, zooming in on the woman just in time to see her vanish inside the squat. He keeps the camera trained on the entrance, for how long he isn't quite sure, until the doors open and two figures burst out. The cheap auto-focus mechanism on the camera can't quite settle on its target in the low light, the digital zoom making the image he is presented with sparkle with pixels.

But it isn't Katja or Miss Pink, instead two men, or teenagers more likely, one dressed in skinny trousers and a t-shirt, the other in cargo pants and an oversized hoody. They hurry away from the place and so Moonbeam puts the camera down. He looks at his watch, cursing the fact that under normal circumstances he'd be tucked up in the comfort of his own bed by now, his wife's warm body next to him. He thinks of the other warm body which was, only a short while earlier, pressed against him but pushes the thought away.

Then the door flies open again and this time it's Miss Pink and she is half-carrying, half-dragging someone behind her. Moonbeam grabs the camera again and points it in the woman's direction. Once more the auto-focus whines in protest, dancing between the few points of light it can pick up on, but he gets enough of a view to recognise who she has in tow, as Katja's shaven head glows with the reflected light. He follows Miss Pink back to her car and for the second time that night watches her stuff the punk's limp body into it. And for the second time that night he follows after her, headlights off, for a dozen or so blocks, pulling his car over when he sees the brake lights ahead.

He isn't familiar with the area, but it's nowhere near the club so where is she taking the punk now?

He watches Miss Pink get out and recover Katja's body from the back seat and it's only then that it strikes him that she might already be dead. He trains the camera on them, following them until they duck into an alley.

There's a moment's hesitation in which he asks himself again whether that would be enough for Kohl, and the answer comes as quickly as before. He jumps out of his car and jogs along the deserted street, and then, the camera still in hand, leans around the alley's corner only as far as he dares.

He spots the van parked three quarters of the way up and instantly recognises the transvestite who first confronted Katja back at the warm up gig. She is locked in conversation with Miss Pink but the two are maintaining a healthy distance, edging around one another like two wild animals that don't want to get into a fight but are entirely prepared for it should it be necessary.

He kneels down, using a pile of rotten fruit crates for cover, dials Kohl's number and quickly updates him.

"So what are they doing? Can you see?"

"They're just . . . talking."

"This is taking too fucking long, I'm sick of it," Kohl snaps. "Give the cop a call. Now."

"But, I mean, it looks like—"

"I've not got time for a game of pass the shitting parcel here, I want that little bitch dealt with, do you understand me? Call him. Call him right now and tell him to get down there fast if he wants a piece of her and make sure he gets her, do you understand? I want to know that she made it into his hands."

Moonbeam no longer has the energy to argue or to question. He feels the strings Kohl is tugging on him, pulling him this way and that in the man's little game of revenge and any resentment is lost amidst the tiredness, amidst the knowledge that he should never have started fucking around with the Nurse Trixie in the first place. The Universe guided him away from her that first night when he scalded his ass against a heating pipe in the closet in which they first fucked and he ignored it—and look where it had gotten him.

So he does as instructed, hoping that perhaps this is the Universe offering him a chance back onto the right path. He makes the call. He tells the cop about the exchange and he just goes along with it when the man assumes him to be some sort of street-smart informant and as he hopes and waits for the man to arrive Moonbeam makes a promise to himself that it is all over with Nurse Trixie. With *all* of them.

And he waits, hiding just around the corner from the white van, praying that the Tgirl won't leave just yet when a battered old station wagon pulls up. A man gets out wearing a raincoat and Moonbeam points the camera—capturing the man sneaking up on the transvestite and felling her, then opening the van doors. Katja emerging and trying to escape but being caught and dumped into the rear of the station wagon.

So that's it. The detective has her and Moonbeam has the proof. Kohl will, finally, be happy.

Moonbeam looks up at the vast darkness twinkling with stars above him, and thanks it, and walks away.

66.

And everything is fine until he rides the elevator down, thinking about getting home and lying down in his own bed next to his wife, about letting the night's events unravel from his muscles, and the elevator doors open and she is standing there.

The punk is standing right there.

67.

"Move me closer," Kohl says, not taking his eyes from Katja in the bed next to him.

Moonbeam pokes the tip of his foot down on the chair's locking mechanism then pushes the man as close to the bed as the contraption will allow. Close enough that she will feel the warmth of his breath on her forehead.

"No. Take this fucking headset off, it's annoying the hell out of me."

Moonbeam does as instructed. "Better?"

Kohl ignores the question, his attention focused on Katja. "Been a while," he says.

"Yeah," she says to him, working against the restraints. "You look . . . different. Have you done something with your hair?"

His smile falters momentarily but he forces it to return. "You know, for a good while there I wished that you had done a better job on me back on the boat. The doctors said that if the cut had been another few millimeters deeper then it would have been a different story. Instead of instant death I ended up with more pain than you can imagine and the ability to move nothing more than this little finger."

He wiggles the digit just to prove his point. "Stuck staring out that window all day and then what do I see? You think a shaved head and a couple of new tattoos is enough? You should never have crawled out from the rock you were under, Katja."

"If it means that much to you, give me a knife and I'll have another go," Katja says.

"No," Kohl says. "It's my turn now. Nurse?"

Moonbeam lingers between the door and the bed to which Katja is strapped. "Look this is . . . I've done enough. I told you already I wouldn't—"

"And *I* told *you* that you would do as I *fucking* asked if you know what's good for you. Prep her."

"No," Moonbeam says, "this isn't right."

"Prep what?" Katja asks.

"The Cosmos brought her here, remember. It delivered her right to us. It *wants* us to have her."

Sensing Moonbeam's resistance wavering, either at the holistic crap Kohl was spouting or at his threats, Kohl says again, "*Prep her.*"

"I won't start it," the nurse says, crossing to one of the machines lying dormant against the rear wall and wheeling it back to the bed.

"I'm not asking you to," Kohl tells him. "This is between me and her but I can't do it myself can I? You're here to care for me, that's your job isn't it? To help me do the things I can no longer do for myself? So prep her."

"What are you doing?" Katja asks, tugging at the restraints but getting nowhere.

The nurse flicks a couple of switches on the machine and there is a hiss of pneumatically-driven air. Then he takes a sterile package from a drawer and splits it open to reveal a needle. He plugs the needle into an IV line that runs from the machine and secures it into place.

He presses down on one of her arms, pinning it. "This will only hurt for a moment," he tells her as if this is just a routine procedure. She barely feels a stab of pain as the cannula is inserted, while trying to read the label on the translucent pouch he hooks the IV line up to.

"Now give me the trigger," Kohl says.

Moonbeam hesitates momentarily then unwraps another line from the machine, this one black as opposed to clear, and ending in what looks likes a stubby permanent marker but the tip isn't a pen, it's a button. He glances down at Katja but his eyes are unable to meet hers. He slips the trigger into Kohl's hand, curling the immobile fingers around it to hold it in place.

Kohl caresses the button with his one good finger.

"I'm guessing that's not saline," Katja says, now slumped in the bed from her efforts to wriggle free.

"You guess right," Kohl tells her. His eyes swivel to Moonbeam. "Tape her up. I've heard enough."

At first Moonbeam isn't sure what Kohl means then notices the roll of surgical tape on the instrument trolley next to him. Kohl blinks in affirmation when Moonbeam picks it up. The nurse peels the end away and pushes it towards Katja.

"Don't you fucking d—"

He presses it onto her mouth, white and waxy and too strong for him to tear with his fingers. He opens the slim top drawer of the instrument trolley and takes out a sterile packet containing a scalpel blade, peels open the packet and uses the blade to slice at the surgical tape across her mouth. He applies another two layers, criss-crossing them to create a crooked star shape, one end touching the base of her nose, another the edge of her jaw.

"Perfect," Kohl says. "You can go now."

Moonbeam doesn't move, as if he is an animal who has been caged for so long that it doesn't know what to do with its freedom when offered. "Are you sure? Maybe I should just make sure that—"

"This is between *me* and *her*," Kohl says, his upper lip curling into a snarl.

Moonbeam puts the tape and blade on the trolley and backs away, working the beads around his neck.

"What about the . . . uh . . ."

"The what?" Kohl asks. The neck brace won't let him angle his head enough to see what Moonbeam stands next to but he already knows. The money they had found on Katja.

"You want it?"

"No, I mean, not for myself but perhaps, you know, to keep it safe or if someone's—"

"Take it," Kohl tells him. "What use is it to me anyway?"

"I could hand it into the lost property downstairs or maybe donate it to a charity or something."

Katja grunts and strains against the surgical tape.

"And it's of no use to you now either," Kohl says to her. "*Take it and get out.*"

Moonbeam picks up the loose notes, the scent of

charred metal and beer rising as he shuffles them into order. The guitar she had been carrying lies there too, spattered with her blood from their struggle in the elevator.

He hears a click as Kohl pushes down on the button beneath his finger, there's an electronic whine, like a small motor spinning up, then a beep and a moment later a muffled gasp from Katja. He stuffs the money into his uniform's chest pocket, and when he stands back up Kohl's face is split by a broad grin.

Moonbeam opens the door and gives Katja one last sorry look before leaving.

He closes it quietly, turns, and then everything falls apart again.

About halfway up the corridor, just beyond the nurse's station, are two people—and both of them trouble. One is the skinny fuckup that had been with Katja by the elevator, the other the Tgirl who had taken Katja's body from Miss Pink in the alleyway, now dishevelled and bloody. They're looking at the patient charts on the wall.

"Oh frick," he says, the words already spoken before he is able to snuff them out.

He ducks back inside Kohl's room in time to hear the click of the man delivering another dose of drug into the punk.

"I thought I told you to—"

"We have a problem."

"What kind of problem?" Kohl asks.

"The cross-dressing kind. The one from earlier. And the guy she was with," he adds, pointing at Katja.

"They followed you here?"

"No! I was careful, I made sure that—"

"Then go deal with them."

"*Me?* What am I supposed to do?"

"*Deal with them!*" Kohl shouts, his eyes wide with fury and the fear of losing everything he has so carefully worked towards. He wants to deliver another dose into the punk's veins but he can't concentrate, and if he can't savour it then what's the point?

Footsteps outside then the outline of two figures in the little rippled glass window on the door. Too petrified to move, Moonbeam grabs the first thing he sees, a fire extinguisher mounted on the wall next to him, and then the door opens and a gun appears, held out by a bloodied and manicured hand. He pins himself back against the wall, hidden behind the now-open door, lets the Tgirl enter and just as she starts to speak he smashes the extinguisher down on her arm. She grunts and the weapon clatters to the waxy floor and he lashes out again, this time connecting with the side of her head. She follows after her gun.

He steps around the door and the skinny one is just standing there, mouth open, so Moonbeam shoves the rounded end of the extinguisher into his stomach. The man crumples and Moonbeam hits him again, this time across his back, and one body on the floor now becomes two. Moonbeam pushes the door shut and locks it this time, and quickly backs away from the bodies towards Kohl. He looks at the fire extinguisher with an expression which suggests that he has no idea of how it go there or why it is shiny with fresh blood and he drops it. It hits the ground with a deep *thud* and rolls away.

The skinny one groans, his face crumpled in pain as he attempts to sit up and fails.

"Get the gun," Kohl says and Moonbeam does as instructed. It shudders and shakes in his grasp as if he is missing the necessary digits to properly grip it. He points it at the two intruders, sweeping it the short distance between one and the other.

"Don't move," Moonbeam says as the skinny one manages to get to his knees. Shards of his black hair flop over his face but even through that jagged veil Moonbeam can see the shock on the man's face when he looks up at Katja and Kohl.

"Well, well, well," Kohl says. "Look who it is. I should have guessed you'd still be following her around like a puppy. Looks like this is going to be even better than I hoped."

The skinny one looks from Kohl to Katja and back again.

"Probably you never thought you'd see me again, right Nikolai?" Kohl says.

Moonbeam trains the gun on the man, not sure if he should have a better understanding of what was going on or not—and not sure if he really wants to know. All he wants now is to get out of there.

"What do we do now?" he asks.

Kohl's eyes go to the slumped figure of Lady D, completely unmoving and now surrounded by a small but growing puddle of blood.

"Just go," Kohl tells Moonbeam. "Get out of here."

"What about him?" Moonbeam asks, nodding at Nikolai.

Kohl smiles broadly. "This useless lump? He's not going to do anything. Are you Nikolai? You're good for nothing. And if you *do* try anything then I'm going to pump her full of more drugs than you've consumed in your entire *life*—and that's saying something, isn't it?"

Nikolai nods.

The gun shudders in Moonbeam's hands. He has to fight with all his power to hold it straight. "So I can . . . go?"

"I have everything I need here," Kohl says, still smiling down at the skinny one.

So Moonbeam backs away towards the door, fumbling for the handle behind him—and steps outside.

68.

It feels like a bomb has gone off in his stomach, not unlike the pain he had suffered during one previous withdrawal bout, but condensed to a few moments rather than the couple of weeks. He tries to pull himself upright a few times before finally managing it through a fog of sparkling lights that blossom and bloom in his vision. When he looks up, there's a man there holding a gun over him and Nik recognises him as the one who grabbed Katja in the elevator.

"Don't move," the man tells him shakily, as if it were even possible for Nikolai to do so in that moment.

And it's not just the pain and disorientation which roots him to the spot, which paralyses him—it's the sight of both Katja gagged and bound to the bed with cable ties, and the man in the disability chair next to her. Nikolai had almost managed to convince himself that it was a mistake or a coincidence, Vladimir Kohl's name on the boards outside, or perhaps a relative out for revenge, or even someone who had assumed the man's identity.

But despite the cocoon of electronics and support devices that encompass the man there is no doubt in Nikolai's mind of who it really is. Kohl tells the nurse to go and the man does so, leaving Nikolai alone in the room with Katja and the body of Lady D. And Kohl.

His limbs are strapped to the chair with thick black rubber straps and they each have a wasted quality to them, the hospital-issue pyjamas hanging from them. A neck brace holds his head upright, squeezing his cheeks up towards his eyeballs. The only thing that moves is one finger, tap-tapping on the little plastic shelf it rests on, all of his tics condensed into one. In his hand is something small and dark.

"So what did you think you were going to achieve coming here exactly, Nikolai?" Kohl asks. "Was that supposed to be your big moment? Rush in here and rescue her? Don't be fucking ridiculous."

Nikolai pushes himself a little more upright, looking at Katja for a sign of what he should do but she just looks back, shakes her head.

"If you're thinking of trying anything then don't bother," Kohl says. "You see that IV line in her arm? It's connected to this little device in my hand which in turn is connected to that machine over there. I press this button and it delivers a little cocktail of drugs straight into her. Do you want to know how I know this, Nikolai? Tell me you want to know."

Nikolai says nothing.

"I know because I was hooked up to it for the first few months I was here. I was in such agony after what you did to me that they had to connect me so that I could deliver my own pain relief as and when I needed it. The machine has safeguards, of course, otherwise patients like me might just keep clicking until the drug has pushed out what little life is left in them. But the safeguards can be switched off."

Kohl's eyes glisten, the faintest smile on his face. His finger stops *tap-tapping*. He presses the button on the device in his hand and there's a whirr then a beep. On the bed Katja stiffens and a few moments later her back arches. She hisses, struggling against the cable ties.

"It's okay, Nikolai. I don't hold you responsible like I do her. You're too much of a fuck-up to have had any real involvement aren't you? Just dragged along for the ride?"

He clicks the button again, whirr-beep, and Nikolai starts towards Katja but Kohl shouts at him to stop. Katja grunts through the tape.

"Don't worry," Kohl says. "It isn't going to be over with quickly. Relatively speaking."

Next to Nikolai, Lady D stirs. She groans, unfolds herself slowly. Blood drips from a gash across one side of her shaven head and her eye is starting to swell. She sits upright, blinking as she takes in the room around her—Nikolai frozen to the spot beside her, the punk girl strapped to the bed and hooked up to an IV drip and the guy in the chair half-consumed by machinery with some sort of trigger device in one hand. She touches the side of her head, examines the blood left behind on her palm and fingers from doing so, looks at the fire extinguisher lying on the floor.

She gets to her feet, using the adjacent wall to steady herself.

Nikolai feels a momentary hope, realising that Kohl is probably now regretting being so quick to get rid of Moonbeam so that he could get down to enjoying himself in private

"Don't do anything stupid," Kohl says warily. His finger flexes over the button on the top of the trigger device. "This doesn't concern you."

"Where's my money?" is all she asks. And Nikolai's hope sinks.

"It just walked out of here," Kohl tells her.

The debt collector looks at the door, a line of smeared blood leading out into the corridor beyond. Her blood. Nikolai catches her eye, silently imploring her to stay and help, but she turns away.

"Thank you," she says to Kohl, then closes the door behind her and leaves the rest of them to it.

69.

Nikolai stares at the door long after the locking mechanism has clicked shut and the shadow of the debt collector has gone from the window.

"That's better, a little privacy for us to share this special moment," Kohl says, the momentary fear that Lady D was going to interfere with his plans now gone. "Poor thing. I think she needs another hit."

He clicks the delivery mechanism and a dose slides up the IV and into Katja. She jerks against the cable ties, her head lolling to one side so that she looks straight at Nikolai.

"Stop it," Nikolai says, crouching with his palms planted on the ground.

"*Stop it?*" Kohl mocks. "No. I don't think I will."

It's as he clicks the mechanism again that Nikolai leaps up, charging at the bed to which Katja is strapped. He he stumbles and collides with an instrument trolley, both he and it slamming into the gurney, the trolley spilling its contents across the bed and onto the floor. Nikolai tumbles over it and onto the bed, onto Katja, then slides off again and crashes to the ground.

And all the while Kohl clicks the feed line, clicks it.

Kohl laughs, tells Nikolai to back away from her once more.

"Was that it? That's the best you've got? That was the most pathetic attempt at heroism I've ever seen," he says. "You are, and always will be, nothing but a useless *fucking* junkie, Nikolai—do you understand that? Tell me you understand that."

Nikolai nods, removing himself from the mess he has created.

"Say it."

Nikolai looks at Katja, her eyes heavy and having difficulty focusing.

"*Say it.*"

"I'm nothing but a useless fucking junkie," he says.

And Kohl smiles—then delivers another dose.

70.

After leaving the room, Lady D looks down the corridor to her left towards the entry doors. They're still barricaded shut but they're being pounded upon, muffled voices and crackling radio-speak audible from beyond. He can't have gone that way. To her right the corridor leads past several doors to a dead end, a small wall decorated with emergency procedure posters and pamphlets for counselling services.

She walks quietly away from the main doors, listening for sounds other than those of life support equipment coming from the rooms beyond then notices one door which is slightly open. It looks like some sort of storage closet, nestled between two of the ward rooms, the scent of disinfectant emerging from within. She slows, listens, then hears a noise coming from inside.

A sudden crash comes from Kohl's room and something which could have passed for guilt momentarily crosses her but she swats it away to focus on the task at hand. Her head throbs, her entire body aches, and that shower is further away than ever—but she still has a job to do.

She quietly opens the door of the closet and finds the nurse bent over before her, clawing at the ground. He's facing away from her, having pushed aside some cardboard boxes and a stack of mops to expose the floorboards beneath, one of them pulled up and a dim light emanating from the gap which has opened.

The gun sticks out of his trousers. Her gun.

The money is stuffed into his uniform's small pockets. Her money.

She snatches the weapon from him before he even realizes she is there. He spins around and it only takes him a split second to realize how much shit he is in. His hands go up in submission, the gun now pointed at him.

"W-w-wait," he pleads, shuffling on his knees to face her. "I didn't . . . isn't my fault—"

"My money," she says simply.

The thudding against the ward's entrance grows louder and there are electronic beeps, perhaps security is now trying to bypass the door locks.

"Listen, this is the only way out of here," the nurse says, nodding at the gap in the flooring. "There used to be an old stairwell here but it was blocked off years ago. They built these storage closets in the space that was left behind, one on each level but you can still . . . if you lift the boards you can get down into the closet on the level below. We could split the money and . . ."

Lady D levels the gun at his head.

There's a crash and Lady D affords a brief glance back down the corridor. Something is being slammed against the doors and a crack appears across one of them. The chairs hold but she doesn't know for how much longer.

"Okay, okay," the nurse says, frantically pulling the notes from his pockets and spilling them onto the floor before him. "The Universe brought the money to me back there and I thought maybe it was just a reward for . . . for what I'd done but obviously it wants you to have it now but that's okay because, you know, these things are planned, we're just cogs, beautiful little cogs but there's a plan, man, I mean ma'am, and it's all . . . it's all just laid out you know?"

Lady D says nothing, keeps the gun trained on him.

"Go on, take it, I didn't really want it anyway," he says to her, shoving the notes towards her but still she doesn't move. She looks at them as if it were his own feces the man was offering her. "Go on, it's what you wanted isn't it? It's what you came for? Ma'am? Look, I j-just want you to know that none of this was my fault. Everything is just a series of events chained together by the Universe, you know?"

Lady D nods. "It's all about the Universe," she says.

"Right!" the nurse says, relaxing slightly now that she understands.

"Yeah," Lady D says. "Which is funny because you know what?"

The nurse shakes his head.

"I've got a black hole for you right here."

And she pulls the trigger.

71.

For a long time she just stares at the body.

Blood spreads out from the wound in the man's forehead, rolling towards the crack in the floorboards which he had started to open up. It sinks into the grain, leaving a glistening sheen. Lady D pushes the nurse to one side with her foot and he slumps onto his back, his eyes open and the goofy, spaced-out look now there in perpetuity.

The money he'd been offering her, *her* money, the money she has been chasing all day and all night lies scattered on the floor next to him. Wet with fresh blood. She crouches down and picks it up, sorts through the notes, separates them where they have clotted together. Her fingers are sticky now too and when she looks at them, it's as if they belong to someone else.

Is this what it comes to? she asks herself. *Scavenging bloody notes like a junkie slurping up the remainder of everyone else's coke?*

There's another *thud* on the ward doors, another *crack*. Someone shouting through the gap which must have opened up. *The Policie are on their way*, they say. And from Vladimir Kohl's room, the whirr-beep of the IV delivery mechanism as the man, presumably, brings the punk closer to her own death.

Kneeling in the puddle of blood, Lady D lets out a long, deep breath.

Her tiredness is a blanket that has been thrown over her, something weaved from the heaviest material known to man, pressing down on her, crushing her. Her head throbs from where she had been struck by the fire extinguisher, her vision blurry. Her arms ache, her feet ache, her back aches.

She has the money and she has her escape route but she just can't bring herself to move.

72.

"*Stop!*" Nikolai shouts, rooted to the spot a couple of feet from Katja's bed and the toppled instrument trolley, as if there were an invisible wall stopping him from getting any closer.

"Or what?" Kohl asks, triggering the IV line for the fourth or fifth time since Lady D left the room. Katja's breathing is laboured, her writhing sluggish and constant, interrupted only by the sudden massive twitches which wrack her body with each dose pumped into her.

Nikolai steps around the end of the bed towards Kohl on the other side but the man calls for him to come no farther, clicks again and again. Katja's making choking sounds now. Her eyes roll back into her head.

"If I jumped you there's nothing you could do," Nikolai says but his words lack intent.

"Of course there is," Kohl tells him, fingering the trigger.

"That's security," Nikolai says when muffled shouts come from the corridor is outside. "The duty nurse managed to trigger an alarm when the debt collector and I broke in. They'll be here any minute."

"You think I care about that?" Kohl says. "You think I care about anything else other than making this bitch suffer? Well I don't, Nikolai. I don't."

"I don't believe you. I think you've been dreaming of getting out of here for months and you're not going to give that up just so you can get your revenge on her."

"You're wrong—that was the only thing I wanted out *for*," Kohl says and, as if to prove his point, clicks the trigger again.

Whirr-beep. Katja's body spasms. Her struggles are lessening, her breathing growing more and more shallow.

Nikolai takes another step closer.

"Stay where you are. I mean it."

"The thing is, you're wrong too, Kohl."

"How's that?"

"You think that she really matters to me? She's the one that got me in this mess in the first place. She dragged me to the mainland then dropped me when I was no longer of any use to her and then just when I thought I was sorting things out she comes crashing back in again. What the fuck do I care what happens to her?"

"You care."

"Yeah?" Nikolai says and takes another step forwards. Only a few feet away from Kohl now, the man helpless in his chair.

"Don't bluff, Nikolai, it doesn't suit you." He clicks the trigger again.

More banging and crashing from outside, more shouting.

"Just get it over with so that I can get out of here before they break in," Nikolai says.

Another step.

"Back!" Kohl shouts, panicking now, clicking the trigger over and over so quickly that it doesn't have time to properly reset itself each time. *"Nikolai!"*

And then Nikolai stops. Holds up his hands, fingers spread.

On the bed beside them, Katja is utterly still. She's stopped responding to the delivery of the doses. Eyes closed, body limp. Kohl is out of breath from the strain and effort. Sweat rolls across his furrowed brow, down across his face and onto the neck brace.

A tired smile spreads across his lips as he looks at Katja and for a while that is all there is in the room— Katja's stillness and Kohl's smile.

13.

Until, a few moments later, she opens her eyes.

Looking right back at Kohl, they're not bleary or confused as he would have expected but as lucid as he has ever seen them. She pulls herself up onto one elbow.

She shouldn't be able to move that far. The cable ties

. . .

Kohl presses the trigger again. The delivery mechanism whirrs and beeps.

She sits up farther, holds one wrist up for him to see. It is raw and inflamed but no longer bound.

Click. Whirr. Beep.

With her freed hand Katja picks up a scalpel blade from the bed and slices through the other cable tie.

Kohl clicks again. And again. He looks at Nikolai who is just standing there, unconcerned. Clicks again.

Katja peels away the surgical tape from her mouth, pulls herself upright, swivels her legs around and off the gurney.

Click. Click. Click.

Kohl doesn't understand it, sweat now streaming down his face.

Click. Click. Click.

She stands right beside him now. Reaches down and picks up the IV line which is plugged into the delivery machine, feeding it through her hand like a sailor would a rope, only when she gets to the end it's no longer plugged into the back of her hand.

She reaches out to Kohl, his eyes going wide with panic, and tips his head down, maneuvering it so that he can see properly.

So that he can see what she has done.

74.

It feels as if her head is being wrapped in thicker and thicker layers of translucent cotton wool, the world around her growing fuzzy and distant and if she's going to get out of there she's going to need to do something soon as whatever it is that Kohl is pumping into her is threatening to overwhelm her.

"It's okay, Nikolai. I don't hold you responsible like I do her," Kohl is saying.

The machine she is hooked up to whirr-beeps and she counts the two seconds it takes for the hit to reach her, bracing herself for its cold entry into her veins. It comes just as Nikolai shouts for Kohl to stop.

Then she's aware of another figure, the debt collector getting to her feet, blood trickling across her head. Kohl's saying something to her. Katja forces herself to focus, catching Nikolai's attention. Her eyes go from him to the instrument trolley beside her, the one which has a line of instruments lined up on it—now including the bare scalpel blade the nurse had used to cut the surgical tape he applied to her mouth. She tugs on the cable tie binding the wrist nearest Nikolai, flexing her fingers to draw attention to it.

Then the debt collector is standing by the door. She makes the briefest of eye contact with Katja before leaving the room and then it's just her, Nikolai and Kohl.

"Poor thing", Kohl says mockingly, "I think she needs another hit."

One second, two seconds, then another cold surge floods into Katja. Nikolai asks the man to stop, and it's as Kohl clicks on the mechanism again that Nikolai leaps forwards, crashing into the instrument trolley and flopping onto Katja's bed before sliding off and crumpling to the ground. Kohl is laughing, mocking Nikolai but it doesn't matter.

She can feel the coolness of the scalpel blade beneath the tip of one finger, grabbed and dropped there by Nikolai. She looks at Kohl to make sure he hasn't spotted the blade but the neck brace keeps his gaze fixed several inches too high. She has to stretch to reach it and for a moment thinks that it's too far away, but she manages to use her middle and ring finger to slide it close enough to grab. She works it into a better position then curls her wrist as far as she can, and starts sawing at the plastic cable tie. She finishes the job, the cable tie snapping open. Checks again that Kohl hasn't noticed but he's too busy antagonising Nikolai. Nikolai notices, however, her hand slipping between the metal guard rail of the bed, leaning on the IV line momentarily so that it pops free, a little translucent snake with a single, huge fang.

"I'm nothing but a useless fucking junkie," Nikolai is saying, his head dipped low in shame. Kohl smiling at him.

Katja, keeping her hand low and out of Kohl's line of sight, reaches farther through the bed rail then stabs the needled end of the line deep into Kohl's thigh. For an instant she is certain that he will cry out in pain, the extent of his condition a lie or an exaggeration, that he will leap from the chair and finish her off in a fury— but there's no reaction. There really is no feeling for him beneath his neck.

Kohl clicks the trigger and the machine *whirr-beeps* again—only this time, although she finds herself bracing instinctively, the sounds aren't followed by a flood of coldness and disorientation.

Nikolai moves around the end of her bed, towards Kohl. "If I jumped you there's nothing you could do," he says.

"I think you've been dreaming of getting out of here for months and you're not going to give up hope on that just so that you can get your revenge on her," he says. Keeping his attention. Riling him.

Kohl tells him he's wrong and clicks the trigger again. Katja plays along, stiffening her body, faking spasms for good measure, making sure her arm doesn't move far from the position in which it should be secured. Nikolai keeps getting closer and closer to Kohl, threatening him, cajoling him. Kohl clicks again. Katja fakes it again, closing her eyes now.

"Back!" Kohl shouts, panicking now, clicking the trigger over and over. The IV machine makes a grinding noise.

Katja keeps her eyes closed, letting Kohl deliver dose after dose into own bloodstream, wondering how long it will take for him to feel the effects or if the damage to his brain will prevent him even sensing anything. Then it's quiet. She hears Kohl panting. He's stopped clicking. She gives him a few moments of belief that he has done what he was so desperate to do before snatching it from him again when she opens her eyes and sits upright.

He keeps pressing the trigger and she lets him, then shows him what she has done—shows him the IV line spiked into his right thigh.

When his expression changes it's like a strange flower blossoming—the shock and terror which replaces the anger and confusion emerging slowly, rather than instantaneous. And once this has happened it's like a cascade, the drugs that he has been pumping himself full of for the last few minutes suddenly overwhelming, his hatred of her inverted and turned in upon himself, his damaged neurons firing belatedly to warn him of the danger.

His eyes go wide, his mouth opens. His finger twitches on the trigger.

It's too late. His system is flooded and he knows it.

His breathing grows ragged.

His eyes are now wider than should be possible, swivelling around, his lids flickering over them. He tries to say something but the words won't come out. Katja and Nikolai, they just look at him.

Then Nikolai leans in close. "Not bad for a useless fucking junkie," he says.

And the muscles in Kohl's face spasm—then everything stops.

75.

"Let's get out of here," Katja says, striding past Nikolai.

She rounds the bed and as she reaches for her guitar the room around her shifts and she tips forwards, crashing into the wall. Nikolai hurries across to help her up but she waves him away.

"I'm fine," she says. She blinks, her vision swimming from the initial dose of chemicals Kohl pumped into her, focussing on the guitar. It's charred, the neck fractured, most of the strings gone. She knows how it feels.

The strap, however, is still intact and so she slips it over her neck, pinning the instrument close to her body, more to stop it from falling to pieces than for security. She steps into the corridor outside then freezes.

"What is it?" Nikolai asks, peering over her shoulder.

Up ahead a gap has been opened between the double doors that provide the only entrance to the ward and a set of hydraulic claws, of the type used to pry a victim out of a crashed car, are currently widening it.

The two turn and head in the opposite direction

sweeping past another dozen or so rooms before reaching the end of the passageway.

"There must be another way out," Katja says, checking the doors one by one but only finding empty intensive care suites.

There's a loud hiss then the sound of metal creaking. More thuds against the double doors.

"*Shit.*"

She turns back.

"Where are you going?" Nikolai asks.

"I don't—"

And she's stopped again.

A few metres ahead Lady D stands before them, the door to the storage closet she has just stepped out of open, her shaven head dark with blood and gun in her hand.

76.

Behind the debt collector is the body of the nurse who attacked Katja and dragged her up into Kohl's room. He is prostrate, a bindi-style bullet wound in his forehead glistening with the blood clotting within it. Money is scattered around him and a couple of the floorboards beneath him have been pulled away to reveal a dim light below.

"Help me move him," Lady D says.

Katja. "And I should help you, why?"

"Because I have a gun aimed at you."

"I'm getting used to it," Katja says, shrugging. "Anyway, where were you five minutes ago when that nutbag had me strapped to the bed?"

"I'm here now. I don't owe you anything."

"And now I don't owe *you* anything," Katja counters, nodding at the money.

"Fine," the debt collector says tersely, pulling the nurse's body up and hooking her arms under him. She drags him back into Kohl's room, Katja watching through the open door as the body is dropped and the gun rested in its lax grip.

"They can draw their own conclusions," Lady D says when she comes back out. She breezes past the two and back into the closet, pulling up another floorboard with her bare hands. She sits on the floor, takes off her heels, and swivels her legs through the gap.

"You coming or not?" she asks.

And Katja thinks of the other transvestite hoodlums from the gig, waiting down there for her, ready to grab her when she is in the middle of dropping herself down and unable to do anything about it.

"We'll manage," she says.

"Really? This is the only way out unless you think you can get past the ones currently trying to break those doors in."

There's a high-pitched pneumatic whine, the amplified cousin of the sound the machine that had almost killed her made, as the claw-device peels back the metal of the doors like they were a food wrapper.

"Hey!" someone shouts and a torch beam sweeps across the polished floor. "Stay where you are!"

"She's right," Nikolai says. "There's no other way out."

"And I'm not waiting for you. You do what you like," the debt collector says, then drops through the gap she has opened up. Katja looks in to see what looks like another storage closet beneath, nobody else visible.

The sounds of metal tearing cease and the voices are louder now. Then maybe footsteps.

"Katja . . ."

"Go!" she says suddenly, pushing Nikolai towards the gap.

He lowers himself in then drops through, landing with a thud and looking up at her expectantly. She lowers her guitar down to him then follows him through while hanging by her hands, draggings the loose boards back into close to their original position. It won't fool anyone for long, but it doesn't have to. She lets go and drops to the ground just as the Policie burst through up above.

77.

"Where did she go?" Nikolai asks.

"I don't see her," Katja says as they cautiously emerge from the closet. The silent passageway extends out on either side of them then a Policie officer appears at one end and instantly they are on the run again.

He shouts after them as they disappear deeper and deeper into the hospital, finally pushing their way through a door marked *Maintenance Staff Only* then down a set of metal stairs, turning and turning on itself before emerging into a large, darkened room filled with boxes. There's a light at the far side and Katja chases it down, Nikolai right behind her.

They emerge onto a loading bay, a concrete platform eight or nine feet above the ground. They drop down and pin themselves to the wall, listening for the sounds of the officer chasing them. Rain is falling heavily, crashing all around them and mixing with pools of engine oil.

Once they feel it's safe they edge their way up the

short alleyway and they're almost at the exit when the patrol car swerves around the corner in front of them.

It revs its engine and speeds towards them.

78.

Before they can react, the car screeches to a halt a metre or so away and the door opens.

When Katja realizes that the person who steps out is Lady D she doesn't know whether it's better or worse than the Policie officer she expected.

"If you want to make it out of here get in the car. You've turned down my help once already—don't do it again."

"Until only a few minutes ago you were after me just like all the others."

"I wasn't after you, I was after my money—and now I have it. Are you getting in or not?"

This time the decision is easier to make.

Katja and Nikolai both climb in the back, finding the unconscious form of a Policie officer already there.

"You might want to dump that," the debt collector says.

Katja reaches across and opens the other door then shoves the man out, slams the door shut again. Lady D throws the car into reverse and backs it out of the alley towards the main hospital car park.

Beyond, more patrol cars are visible, their lights flickering off the nearby buildings, some parked, others circling slowly . A row of them are blocking the main exit from the hospital grounds.

"Is his hat still there?" Lady D asks.

Katja picks it up from the back seat and hands it over. Lady D puts it on then sticks the car back into gear and slowly trundles towards the road block. One of the officers manning it looks up when they see the other vehicle approaching, squinting to identify their colleague behind the wheel, relaxed enough that he doesn't unhook his thumbs from his belt.

Lady D keeps it slow, hits the button to roll the driver's side window down and as they draw nearer the officer leans in to speak to them. It's as he does this that Lady D suddenly revs the engine and the patrol car pitches forwards, slamming into two of the other cars just at the point where they meet. She keeps the revs high until it pushes through, the officer still fumbling to free his gun from its holster when then the car finally breaks free and speeds off.

79.

Katja and Nikolai do their best to stay upright in the back seat as the car swerves from side to side, threatening to topple over as the debt collector throws it around corners without braking. There are sirens in the near-distance and the call for help to the other patrol cars crackles through the radio mounted on the dashboard.

Lady D soars through a red light at a junction, narrowly missing a car coming in the opposite direction, before the flashing lights of another patrol car appears behind them. Its siren blares at them and it attempts to slide up beside them, but Lady D swerves away, so it swings to the other side, this time connecting its nose to their tail. Sparks from the point of contact flash against the window next to Katja, and then they are sent into a spin. The neon glare of the city whirls around them for a few moments before they come to a sudden stop, slamming into another parked car.

Katja pulls herself upright, Nikolai doing the same beside her, and she looks out to see one corner of the hood crumpled and steam slipping out from the darkness within. Lady D is slumped across the front seats, having been thrown there at the moment of final impact, groaning and clutching a fresh head wound.

"They're coming," Nikolai says, pointing at the headlights approaching them.

Katja jumps through into the front, shoving the debt collector into the passenger seat and restarting the stalled engine. Metal grinds against metal as she searches for a gear, throwing it into reverse and backing away from the oncoming patrol car, locking the steering to swing around in a semi-circle, the red-and-blue flashing past. She forces it into first and accelerates off before their pursuer can correct themselves.

"Two blocks north then a hard left," Lady D says, wiping the blood from her head.

Smoke is now pouring from the front-end of the car and the engine is making a regular clunking noise but it still manages to speed away, the other car now back on their tail.

"Ready?" Lady D says, glancing over shoulder then at Katja. Her hand is wrapped around the handbrake. Nikolai grips his seat.

Katja nods, prepares herself, the patrol car right behind them now, then Lady D pulls on the handbrake and everything is spinning again and the tyres are shrieking. Katja fights with the wheel before steadying it and continuing up the rain-slicked street, leaving the patrol car behind.

"Left again," Lady D says, and Katja does as she says but the car is slowing now, losing power, the clunking from the engine becoming louder and more regular, the steam pouring out thicker and darker.

"Where are we going?"

"Just up ahead, over there."

Katja hears the siren getting closer but there's still no sign of the red and blue lights. She struggles to find a working gear again, maintaining just enough momentum to turn the car past a barbershop with a crumbling sign which reads *Frank's Place* and into the alleyway Lady D has indicated before the engine dies completely. The vehicle drifts for the final few metres before she swings it in behind a graffiti-covered dumpster and brings it to a halt.

They all remain silent and still until the chasing patrol car flashes past, the ghostly ribbons of its lights quickly fading to nothing, then they climb out. Lady D reaches up to a ledge above a shuttered doorway at the rear of the barbershop and takes down a set of keys. She releases a padlock and draws the shutters up, looks back at Nikolai and Katja.

"Stay out here if you like," she says, her sentence punctuated by the timely sounds of more patrol cars getting closer.

Nikolai looks to Katja who considers the situation momentarily before nodding for them to follow the debt collector inside.

Lady D flicks on the lights, revealing the row of ratty red-leather chairs and milky containers of Barbicide. The large mirrors which line one wall reflect the bloodied and bedraggled images of the three standing between yellowing photos of hair models with the vacant smiles of recently-converted Christians. The debt collector goes through a door at the rear, Katja and Nikolai following.

The short, dimly-lit corridor is lined with more badly-framed photos, but instead of cheesy models these all appear to be of clients seated in or next to the barbers chairs out front. They're all signed in thick black ink. Katja recognises some of them as minor celebrities, the rest looking more like mobsters and other hoodlums and in each one is the same man, vaguely muscled and with a shaven head.

She stops for a closer look, then realizes who it is.

At the end of the corridor is a bedroom, the modest bed surrounded by wardrobes and drawer units stuffed full of clothes. Lady D takes off the Policie shirt and peels off her bloodied dress and heels, then kneels down and pushes one of the units to the side. She works a couple of fingers into a gap in the plaster around a heating vent and pulls the metal grille away and reaches inside, all the way up to her shoulders. She grunts and strains before dragging a chunky leather satchel out and dusting it off. Dumps it on the bed and pops it open and it's stuffed with cash.

"So this is who you are when you drop the Lady D act?" Katja asks, pointing to one of the pictures behind her. In it, Frank the barber presently standing before her wearing only a thong and some bruises, has his arm around a young man with the build and egotistical smile of an upcoming sports star.

"You don't get it," Lady D says, putting the money she'd recovered from the nurse into the satchel and zipping it up. She points at the man in the picture. At Frank. "*He's* the act."

Then she pulls open one of the cupboard doors to reveal a dozen or more wigs mounted on foam heads and selects one—ice-blonde, medium length and with a razor-edged fringe—then pulls it on.

"Now hand me that lipstick."

80.

Lady D's uniquely-decorated white van is parked up a little ahead of the stolen patrol car, the dark tarpaulin which had been draped over it now removed to reveal large red lips painted across the rear doors. She opens the doors, parting those lips, throws her satchel and a couple of suitcases she had hurriedly filled into the back.

"So I guess we should be heading off now," Katja says.

Now dressed in a dark purple velvet dress with black lacing at the edges, black stockings and another set of killer heels, Lady D cocks her head to one side.

"Heading where exactly?"

Katja shrugs. "Inland."

"That's your plan, *head inland*? And then what, another gig?"

"What else am I good for?"

"Then I hope you've got someplace safe to go because if you think that Kohl being dead means this whole thing is over with, then you're badly mistaken. Way it seems to me, just about every motherfucker in this city is after you for one reason or another. You start plastering pictures of yourself all over the place again and—"

"I can handle myself."

"Really? How did that work out for you tonight?"

As they talk Lady D retrieves a plastic canister from the back of the van and pours the fuel over the Policie car.

"I'll take my chances. I'm done with hiding. Like you said I had every freak and weirdo after me today . . . no offense . . ."

"None taken."

". . . and I'm still here aren't I?"

"Not without a little help," Lady D says, pointedly glancing at Nikolai, before working the petrol trail towards the barber shop. She then takes a cloth rag from the van and stuffs it into the neck of the canister before lighting it and throwing it through the open doorway of the barbershop. Nikolai takes a few more steps away from the building just as the line of flame flows out of the shop and towards the patrol car.

"You need protection," Lady D says, cleaning her hands on another rag, the fire quickly spreading. "At least to start with. Plus you need a ride and I guess that I'm looking for a new job."

"You're not serious," Katja says, ignoreing the growing heat and the oily smoke spilling out around them.

"You wear heels like these, you're always serious, honey. I can keep you safe—plus I can string a guitar."

"That's more than we can do," Nikolai mutters.

Katja glares at him. "Look, the one person I'm willing to trust is standing right beside me and I'll give you a hint—he's not the one wearing a gaffe."

She's aware of Nikolai giving her a look but ignores it.

"Sweet—but not very sensible," Lady D says.

"I really don't think we should hang around here much longer," Nikolai says, sweat now beading across his brow. There's the sound of glass shattering from inside the barbershop, of metal creaking as it expands. The whine-puff of compressed air as the patrol car tires give way.

"I agree," Lady D says. "So . . . ?"

Nikolai wrings his hands, rocks from one foot to the next. "Katja?"

The same sooty-grimey air which had filled her lungs only an hour or so earlier clots in her mouth, and she thinks of the Wheatsheaf's roof racing towards her.

"Get in the van."

ACKNOWLEDGEMENTS

Thanks to Tiffany "consultant Tgirl" Leigh, Bill "respect the proscenium" Freedman, Bracken "you call that an opiate?" MacLeod and Thomas "kill MacCauley" MacCauley. Thanks also to Agent Al, Brian Lindenmuth and Pork Chop, and to all the folks at CZP, including editor extraordinaire Sam Zucchi, artist extraordinaire Erik Mohr, and just general extraordinaires Brett and Sandra.

And, of course, to Jen, who inspires and guides everything I do—whether she knows it or not.

ABOUT THE AUTHOR

Simon Logan is the author of the short story collections *I-O*, *Rohypnol Brides*, and *Nothing is Inflammable*, and the industrial fiction novel *Pretty Little Things To Fill Up The Void*, as well as *Katja From The Punk Band*. His website is at http://www.coldandalone.com.

EMB
RACE
THE
ODD

DEAD AMERICANS
BEN PEEK

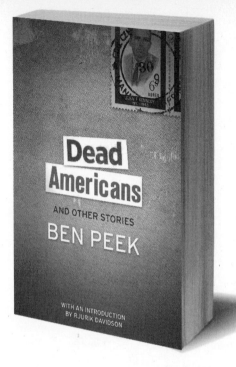

A collection of the critically acclaimed surreal short fiction of Ben Peek. It presents a world where bands are named after the murderer of a dead president, where the work of Octavia E. Butler is turned into an apocalypse meta-narrative, and John Wayne visits a Wal-Mart. It presents a world where a dying sun shines over a broken, bitter landscape, and men and women tattoo their life onto their skin for an absent god. It presents the visions a dreaming Mark Twain has of Sydney, a crime that begins in a mosque, and answers a questionnaire you never read.

AVAILABLE MARCH 2014
978-1-77148-171-7

THINGS WITHERED
SUSIE MOLONEY

For the first time in one collection, award-winning author Susie Moloney unveils thirteen of her most dark and disturbing short stories.

A middle-aged realtor makes a deal that could last forever. A cheating woman finds herself swimming in dangerous waters. A wife with a dark past can't bear the fear of being exposed. The bad acts of a little old lady come home to roost. A young man with no direction finds power behind the wheel of a haunted truck.

From behind the pretty drapes of the average suburban home, madness peers out.

AVAILABLE NOW
978-1-77148-161-8

WILD FELL
MICHAEL ROWE

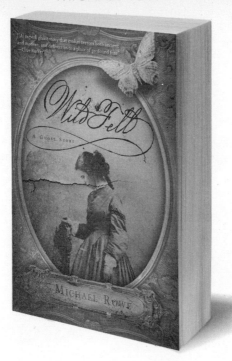

The crumbling summerhouse called Wild Fell, soaring above the desolate shores of Blackmore Island, has weathered the violence of the seasons for more than a century. Built for his family by a 19th-century politician of impeccable rectitude, the house has kept its terrible secrets and its darkness sealed within its walls. For a hundred years, the townspeople of alvina have prayed that the darkness inside Wild Fell would stay there, locked away from the light.

Jameson Browning, a man well acquainted with suffering, has purchased Wild Fell with the intention of beginning a new life, of letting in the light. But what waits for him at the house is devoted to its darkness and guards it jealously. It has been waiting for Jameson his whole life . . . or even longer. and now, at long last, it has found him.

GAMIFICATION /C–MONKEYS
KEITH HOLLIHAN

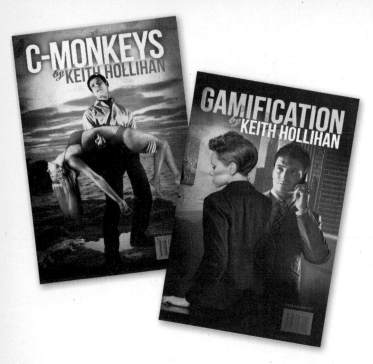

This is a double novella "flip book" pairing a modern corporate suspense story about the cover-up of a CEo's illicit affair, with a 1970s-era science fiction thriller about an oil company's environmental disaster. It is an exploration of the paranoia inherent in business and the thin line between competition and conspiracy.

AVAILABLE NOW
978-1-77148-151-9

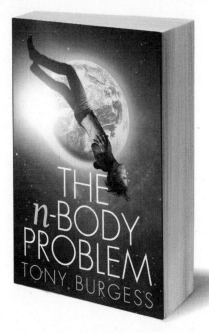

MORE FROM CHIZINE

ALSO AVAILABLE FROM CHIZINE PUBLICATIONS

SWALLOWING A DONKEY'S EYE PAUL TREMBLAY [978-1-926851-69-3]

THE HAIR WREATH AND OTHER STORIES HALLI VILLEGAS [978-1-926851-02-0]

THE WORLD MORE FULL OF WEEPING ROBERT J. WIERSEMA [978-0-9809410-9-8]

WESTLAKE SOUL RIO YOUERS [978-1-926851-55-6]

MAJOR KARNAGE GORD ZAJAC [978-0-9813746-6-6]

"IF YOUR TASTE IN FICTION RUNS TO THE DISTURBING, DARK, AND AT LEAST PARTIALLY WEIRD, CHANCES ARE YOU'VE HEARD OF CHIZINE PUBLICATIONS–CZP–A YOUNG IMPRINT THAT IS NONETHELESS PRODUCING STARTLINGLY BEAUTIFUL BOOKS OF STARKLY, DARKLY LITERARY QUALITY."

–DAVID MIDDLETON, **JANUARY MAGAZINE**

ALSO AVAILABLE FROM CHIZINE PUBLICATIONS